SANDMAN

Sandman

Bob Drews

Writers Club Press
San Jose New York Lincoln Shanghai

Sandman

Writers Club Press
an imprint of iUniverse, Inc.

For information address:
iUniverse, Inc.
5220 S. 16th St., Suite 200
Lincoln, NE 68512
www.iuniverse.com

ISBN: 0-595-20616-6

Printed in the United States of America

To Lisa

Who Filled My Heart,
Found My Soul and Let My Spirit Soar

I Love You

ACKNOWLEDGEMENTS

Stephanie, Larissa and Leo, thank you for being, and for teaching me things I hope you, too, find one day in your hearts.

Mom and Dad, thank you for being there, as parents, guardians and friends.

Lisa, thank you for being here, for being my wife, for loving me and letting me love you.

CHAPTER I

DISCOVERY

"Maybe I should just piss off of the porch."

Phillips smiled to himself. Lying on his back and staring at the ceiling in the bedroom of his childhood, he recalled the times he had stepped outside to pee. Sometimes he had tried to hit birds in the apple tree just beyond the porch railing. Once he had actually tried to swirl the pee so that he could spell his name in the snow below, but the only thing he had managed to do was have his sister Kate yell "It's raining" to their mother as they looked out the kitchen window while doing the dishes. If Mom knew, she never said anything.

Phillips didn't know now, any more than he did then, why he didn't just go downstairs to the toilet like a normal human being. Maybe he was rebellious, maybe creative, maybe just plain lazy. There seemed to be a difference between doing it at 14 and at 48, but at least for the moment it didn't bother him.

"People always tell me I never grew up. Maybe they're right," Phillips said as he opened the door and stepped onto the porch into the bright sunlight of a Midwestern summer day. It was noon and heating up, getting sticky as the folks out here called it, humid as people in the East would put it. Funny that the humidity had never bothered him while growing up in his carefree days of the '50s and early '60s. But now it made him feel just like the word described it. And that was probably why it was called sticky. The people in his adult life on the East Coast always did have a way of using words that failed to describe a situation or put an unnecessary gloss on things. No matter how long he lived in Washington, D.C., Phillips vowed to himself that he would never lose that part of him he held precious from his childhood, to live life directly and to the point. After more than a decade out East, he could say in all honesty that he had made good on his promise. Now, he vowed, this would be more true than ever.

"Tom, everyone will be here in an hour. Start getting ready." His mom's voice, carrying up the stairway to the bedroom, caught Phillips just as he was about to let loose with a stream over the porch. "Damn, a man can't even take a leak in peace," he said half-jokingly, still wondering just why he kept on doing this. Not growing up didn't seem answer enough. Then again, maybe the answer really didn't matter.

"Didn't matter." That was the answer Phillips had used over the years when he couldn't find the answer to something. While some of his friends had to find an answer in everything, Phillips liked the "didn't matter" way out. It was clean and to the point and left no hangups or emotional residue. When he was sad, mad, frustrated, bored, it "didn't matter." When he broke up with a girlfriend, it "didn't matter." When a writing deal fell through, it "didn't matter." And when he pissed from the porch as a grown man, it "didn't matter" either. But the recent events in his life surely did matter, and all the "didn't matters" he said to himself would not take them away. And he knew they never would.

Talking to himself had become as much a part of life for Phillips as shaving. When he talked to himself, "didn't matter" was almost always nearby, just like it was now as he zipped up.

Phillips went back inside and looked around the room. He hadn't lived in this house for over 25 years, though he had come back often for visits. Still, it seemed a little odd that his parents hadn't changed a thing. "You'd think," he said to himself, "they would turn it into a guest room, a TV room, a recreation room, a sewing room, anything other than a bedroom for a boy long since gone." He reasoned that maybe his parents so loved him they couldn't bear the thought of changing the room around, or maybe they just couldn't think of any other use for it. Maybe they wanted to keep the room as Phillips liked it so that when he returned for a visit he would feel at home. And then again, maybe to his parents, it didn't matter either.

He thought about this as he went through the chest of drawers, looking over the things he once held dear. Phillips hadn't gone through these things in years, and what he found made him smile, giving his heart a tug of happy memories. There was an old Montgomery Ward's catalog, the pages for hunting guns dog-eared from the time in high school he had begged for a rifle so he could go squirrel hunting with his friends. Marbles, still in the bag his mom had made for him. A baseball glove, musty and fragile with age.

His high school yearbook, filled with musings from friends long gone and pictures of youth long spent. Even, for God's sake, some clothes from high school, sizes so small he could barely believe he once fit into them.

"Shit, I probably wore some of those pants when I pissed over the porch." He chuckled again.

Phillips loved amusing himself. He could remember as a boy, growing up with just the one sister, that he often had to play by himself, either in the yard on those sticky summer days or down in the basement during the snowy winters. There were trucks and train sets, games of jacks, bouncing a ball off the front porch steps to play an imaginary baseball game. He could remember playing war games in the bathtub, floating the small boats his dad bought him and then bombing them with the soap bar. Phillips was at his best by himself growing up and grown up, and he never felt it to be strange or in any way to diminish himself as a man or a person. He liked to think it meant he was strong.

Nothing was particularly special about Tom Phillips. He had a masculinity that made him moderately handsome, maybe a 6 on a scale of 10. He had high cheekbones, a muscular but not chiseled physique, blue eyes and brown wavy hair with a touch of gray in the back and in the sideburns that made him look old enough that he wasn't feared by women as a man on the prowl and young enough that when he was he didn't go home empty-handed.

He had been blessed with his dad's respect for hard work, discipline and fair play and his mom's gift of graciousness when a soft touch or soothing word was called for. "Joe and Peggy," he had often said to himself and to them, "thank you for being my parents." Sitting on the edge of the bed, Phillips was thinking back on them and growing up in this happy house with Joe, Peggy and Kate when his emotions overwhelmed him yet again. "Dammit, stop. Stop." But it was no use. He could not hold back the tide of melancholy and anger, fear and self-hatred, pity and more pity. The independence and strength he had always taken pride in, had built up for decades had vanished in an instant that afternoon in the doctor's office three weeks and a lifetime ago. Once more, he replayed it in his mind.

"So what's the verdict, doc?" Phillips had asked breezily while his stomach churned with anxiety over the answer he hoped wouldn't come but knew it would. His symptoms had started innocently. Don't they always? He would forget his phone number, not for a long time but just long enough to make him wonder. Then he would have to look up his ZIP code in his notebook even though he had lived at the same address for more than 10 years. Sometimes he got lost driving home. Kate or Bea or his mom and dad would ask him why he was telling them about a trip when he had told them about it just a week before.

Then the mood swings came. For the first time since the hormone-crazed days of his teenage years he would become depressed. Or he found himself disoriented on writing trips to the point he had to go back to his hotel room and take the afternoon off. Sometimes he would call Kate and ask her if he should take an assignment when he had simply said yes or no on his own dozens of times before.

And so began the trail of doctor's visits that ended on a rainy afternoon at the hospital in suburban Washington.

"Tom, I'm sorry, but the tests confirm you have Alzheimer's disease."

Phillips stared at the floor. "You're sure?"

"Yes, Tom. There is no doubt."

Phillips had had enough tests to not question the results as he and the doctor sat in silence. Physical exams, neurological exams, CAT scans, thyroid tests, blood tests, the hospital had done everything but measure his pecker. It was the truth.

Even now, sitting in his bedroom after all that had happened, he could remember the cold, dark reality of that Monday and the thought that went through his mind in the doctor's office: There's nothing I can do about this. Or is there?

C H A P T E R   2

▼

A L O N E

Phillips left the hospital that day and went to see *American Beauty*. He had been to it twice already but wasn't in the mood for any surprise endings just now. He had always found comfort in the movies, as a place to escape, to dream, to sit in the dark, to savor aloneness. But this time the movie did him no good and he left after an hour. Unlikely for him, Phillips, never a man to spend a penny foolishly, had bought a tub of popcorn. "You only live once," he said before taking a mouthful, then running off to vomit. "Great, the one time I spring for popcorn I ended up puking it out," he said as he hung onto the toilet bowl.

Hours later, Phillips woke up. He didn't remember how he got home or even coming home. Somehow he had gotten there, gone to bed and fallen into a sleep that left him lethargic, almost dazed, when he finally came out of it. His clothes were drenched in sweat. The apartment was dark except for a streetlight that cast a single beam into the living room. He could see it through the bedroom door, which he uncharacteristically had left open when he went to bed. Phillips became disoriented, fell onto the floor, curled into a ball and cried. He fell back asleep.

When he awoke again, it was dark like before. He stumbled to his feet and turned on the light beside his bed. It was 11 p.m. Hours had passed since the hospital. "Was it a dream? Am I awake now? Am I dead?"

Phillips sat up and yelled at himself. "I cannot believe this is happening. Get a grip on yourself, you asshole. Stop this. Stop it!"

He reached for the phone. Who to call? There were six people Phillips could reach out to at a time like this: Bea, Helena, Kate, Natalie, Mom or Dad. Bea and Kate were undoubtedly out for the night, Natalie was too young, Helena tucked in with her husband and kids, Mom asleep and Dad put to bed in the nursing home. So there was no one. That was probably better anyway. Who knows what he might say? He didn't know himself.

Maybe then, for the first time, or at least the first time he had seriously thought about it, Phillips realized he was alone because that was the world he had built for himself. The world he prided himself in. Until now it hadn't mattered. "Didn't matter." Funny.

With no one to talk to and nowhere to turn, Phillips forced himself to do something he was good at. Thinking. And so he sat on the floor, elbows on knees, looking off into space and trying to get his bearings.

After a minute or two he came to a conclusion. "I need something to eat." Food was a joy, a tonic and a recreation for Phillips. He wasn't overweight by any means, because while he loved to eat, he didn't overeat. He so savored mouthfuls of food that sometimes he felt ripples of pleasure almost like sexual gratification. Right now he was hungry for a good deli sandwich. The June night in Washington was hot and stifling. Sticky. He quickly went to the living room to turn on the air conditioner.

Wearing cut-off jeans, a T-shirt and sandals, Phillips walked up the stairs from his basement apartment to the street above. His apartment was three blocks from the Capitol. The neighborhood would never win any awards for safety, but it wasn't the slums, and besides, after living here and doing quite a bit of traveling to other big cities, Phillips was street-wise enough to take precautions to keep out of trouble. He jogged the block to the Kashmir Deli, an all-night place that, strangely enough, served huge sandwiches that rivaled any Jewish deli he had ever been to.

"Baloney on a sesame bun, lettuce, dill pickles and mayo," Phillips told Abe, the owner. Phillips knew little about Abe other than that he had come from the Middle East with his wife and two kids, worked monstrously long hours and got the nickname Abe from a customer who said his beard looked like that of another Washington resident of the 1860s. Abe didn't mind, or at least didn't say so, and seemed to be happy if his store simply had a steady flow of customers, which it always did. Even now, near midnight, three other people were there looking at the sandwich board to decide what to buy.

"Tom, how're you doing tonight?"

"A little under the weather, but I'll get by."

Abe knew Tom liked his sandwiches cut in half. "They taste better that way and it just feels like there's more to the sandwich" was Phillips' way of explaining it. Abe had never contested him, and Phillips reasoned it was either because he didn't understand him, agreed with him or thought he was so full of crap it was pointless to try arguing.

With his sandwich and a wave of the hand, Phillips left Kashmir Deli and walked slowly home. Phillips loved Washington, always had, from the first time he visited at age 15 with his parents and Kate on an East Coast vacation. He loved the pace of the city, its history, its proximity to the South and the big cities of the East, its restaurants, its sights and sounds. He could have visited the Smithsonian Institute every day and never tired of it. Long, leisurely walks along the Potomac were an evening staple when he wasn't out of town on assignment doing a travel story. It was perhaps the Potomac that was his single favorite place because from his earliest childhood days, Phillips had loved water. Oceans, lakes, rivers, streams, if it was wet and had waves or flowed, Phillips found peace and tranquillity on its shores or along its banks.

Back in control of himself, at least for the moment, Phillips stopped and felt the heavy air outside his apartment. He could see the dome of the Capitol from here, a sight that always gave him chills of wonder and awe when silhouetted against the night sky. At one time, a long time ago, he had entertained thoughts of going into politics himself, thinking that perhaps after he graduated from college he would return to his home town, get a job and build a life and from there launch a career in state government and then go on to office in Washington. That things hadn't proceeded along this path had never saddened or bothered Phillips, who was never one to look back on missed or untaken opportunities. He had always tried to put one step in front of the other and proceed forward, and his journey had taken him to good places and good people and fit in nicely with his state of mind.

"I never could have put up with all the bullshit from all those voters" anyway, Phillips reminded himself as walked down the steps to his apartment. Turning on the lights in his place always made Phillips feel good. His two-bedroom apartment reflected him, comfortable but not fancy, nice touches but not ostentatious. He had converted the smaller bedroom to a den where he did his writing. The furniture was comfortable and kept in perfect shape. A small bar in one corner of the living room was well-stocked, the sofa luxurious, a hutch in the kitchen proudly displaying china he had inherited from his grandparents. The TV cabinet was a fine mahogany and besides the 25-inch television had a stereo, VCR, CD player and radio. Whenever Phillips returned home, it was his intention to shut out the world, and he had provided himself with the creature comforts to do just that.

This night was no exception. Phillips stripped down to his boxer shorts, set up a TV table in front of the sofa, turned on the ESPN sports highlights and prepared to eat. "Damn this is sweet," he said, the food and TV sweeping away his sorrow, at least for the moment. He got a Coke from the refrigerator, opened a bag of Fritos, put the sandwich on a plate and settled in. Abe had made the sandwich just the way Phillips liked it. Six slices of meat, mayo peeking from the sides of the bun, the pickles sour, the bun just crisp enough that a few crumbs fell to the plate with each bite. Phillips spent half an hour savoring his food and the sports highlights, then turned to a nightly ritual: classical music. Tchaikovsky was his favorite and he fed Symphony No. 6 into his CD player, lay down on the couch and listened to the dark, melancholy strains. How fitting they seemed tonight.

C H A P T E R 3

▼

THE BIBLE

Phillips dozed off for about 20 minutes during the music. When he awoke he shut off the CD player, washed and put away the dishes and tidied up the living and dining room. He refused to ever get up to a dirty house, just as he refused to go to an unmade bed. Phillips had been accused more than once of being zealously neat, but it didn't bother him. In fact he took pride in it. Phillips didn't care what other people thought.

If anyone had ever thought to ask what was the single most important thing to him in life, Phillips would have answered without hesitation: "peace of mind." Routine gave him peace, and reading from the Bible plus one other book, usually a novel, was a nightly ritual. No matter how he felt, spending even a few minutes with his books was enough to ensure a restful, peaceful night of sleep. It had been this way with him for close to 15 years, and he could never conceive of a thing that would make him interrupt this pattern.

He loved mysteries in particular. His novel of the moment was Lawrence Sanders' *McNally's Trial,* a good yarn that usually gave Phillips a chuckle or two. After the novel, he would read the Bible. His Scripture reading was simple. He started with Genesis and read straight through until he finished Revelation, then would go back to Genesis and start all over again. Each night he would read as much as he felt like, sometimes a verse, sometimes a chapter, sometimes more. Phillips was on his fourth reading and always looked forward to the Psalms, whose messages particularly pleased him. Psalm 25 had been his favorite reading from the first time through, and nothing he had read since had displaced it.

Reading the Bible had actually been his mother's suggestion, way back when he was a teenager. Then, of course, he didn't listen. Phillips would wonder from time to time, more out of amusement than anything else, if every man realized at some point in his life how totally full of crap he was at age 17.

Actually at 17 Phillips was an avid reader, of Hustler, Playboy, whatever porn magazine he could get his hands on. Only it wasn't just for mindless gratification. Firm in the belief that exercising any muscle would cause it to grow bigger and stronger, he would wait until his parents and Kate turned out their lights for the night, then would haul out his magazine and let himself get aroused. His reasoning was simple. An erection every night was good exercise for his penis, and therefore it naturally had to grow. He kept a ruler under his mattress along with his magazines and every night would dutifully measure his member and record its length in a notebook he kept nearby. He did this for nine months, and in that time he had grown exactly three-eighths of an inch. If that were due to his exercise master plan or just the normal growth of a teenage boy he could never figure out.

In time he just got bored with the idea and finally quit. Neither of his parents had ever mentioned finding anything under his mattress, so he had presumed all these years that it would forever be his little secret.

Tonight, though, Phillips wasn't ready yet to turn to his books. Before he could rest he would have to consider his options in facing the disease that he knew marked a turning point in his life. Phillips always thought better anyway when he had his thoughts on paper, so he poured himself a cup of coffee and heated it in the microwave, went to his desk in the den and fired up his personal computer. Again, Phillips had a routine. No matter what else his business at the PC, and tonight was no different, he would first surf his favorite Web sites: CNN, ESPN and MSN. He got most of his news from the Internet, generally reading newspapers only for the sports. And even with that, he couldn't get enough sports so he would check into ESPN.com several times a day, eagerly following the home run exploits of Mark McGwire and Sammy Sosa. Phillips prided himself on being more than just another blind follower of who was doing the best, or getting really interested in any sport, particularly baseball, just during the playoffs. Growing up, Hank Aaron was his favorite ballplayer, for the Milwaukee Braves from nearby Wisconsin, but to Phillips whether Hank Aaron or Hank Allen was batting, it was all the same. The love of baseball had stayed with Phillips from childhood, through his college years and into adulthood, the one constant linking him in his 40s to when he was a boy. Phillips had often said to himself and others that when he died, he hoped it was during baseball season.

His Web sites checked, Phillips began to write.

OPTIONS

1. Let the disease run its course, hope for treatment that cures me or at least stops the disease and lets me have a good lifestyle.
2. Wait until the disease starts to get debilitating, then commit suicide.
3. Live with relatives or friends once I become incapacitated.
4. Live in a nursing home once I become incapacitated.
5. Kill myself now.

None of the options looked particularly palatable, but Phillips looked at the last one with some amusement, snorted and said "Yeah, right," before shutting down the computer. This would all have to wait until at least tomorrow when he could face the issue with a clearer mind and would have a chance to talk with his doctor.

Phillips made a mental note to call the doctor's office in the morning to make an appointment, climbed into bed, opened the novel and then, rare for him, quickly put it down. "Not tonight." He opened the Bible instead, where the bookmark was at Joshua, Chapter 16: And the lot of the children of Joseph fell from Jordan by Jericho, unto the water of Jericho on the east, to the wilderness that goeth up from Jericho through mount Bethel.

He turned out the light and went to sleep.

CHAPTER 4

THE DOCTOR

Phillips picked up the phone, dialed two numbers, slammed it back down and yelled, "Dammit!" Up early to make a doctor's appointment, he had started to call, only to realize he couldn't remember the rest of the phone number. A month ago he would have joked about this with his drinking crowd as a "senior moment" or the onset of the "Big A." Now that was not funny anymore. Phillips got out the phone book, looked up the number and wrote it in a new note pad he took from his desk drawer. "Might as well get used to this," he said, his voice a mix of sarcasm and regret.

He dialed again. "Doctor Frank's office," the receptionist answered. "Hi, this is Tom Phillips calling. I wanted to make an appointment with the doctor today if possible."

"Oh, Tom. Thank you for calling. We were worried when you left yesterday. You looked deathly pale and marched right past and out the door. Let me see if doctor can see you today."

Phillips cradled the phone and looked out the window, which like most apartments in this neighborhood had security bars. From his basement apartment he could see the legs of passersby, most of them hurrying past on their way to work on Capitol Hill. Phillips didn't have to open a window or step a foot outside to know it would be hot just like the day before and the day after.

He sat back in his recliner and waited. The receptionist returned. "Doctor can see you at 2 this afternoon, if that works for you."

"I'll be there. And thank you and the doctor for your concern."

Phillips remained in the chair. He was still in boxers, his pajamas of choice during Washington's miserable summers. Helena had given them him these for Christmas, tasteful white cotton shorts decorated with seashells. "I sure hope I see her tonight," Phillips said, surprising himself. It was the first time he had wished to see anyone since yesterday afternoon.

Phillips arose and started on his daily household rounds, getting the paper from just outside the door, pouring a cup of coffee, frying an egg and putting it on an English muffin, lightly toasted, with mayonnaise, dill pickles and a slice of cheese. He settled down at the dining room table with the sports pages, but after taking a bite he looked away, lost in thought.

"What am I to make of this? Everything was going so good and now this happens. I just can't believe this is happening to me.

"God, what am I going to do?"

Since it was only 9:30 Phillips actually was ahead of schedule for the day. Normally a night owl who slept regularly until 10, he would usually get up, eat, read his sports pages, then check for writing assignments or other e-mail messages on his computer.

Phillips was a travel writer, had been one for about 12 years and loved what he did for a living. After so many years in the business, coupled with the good publicity that had come from his successful novel, Phillips had more inquiries than he could handle, putting him in the enviable position of being able to choose which assignments he wanted.

Phillips went into the den, sat at his desk and looked at the calendar. It was Tuesday, June 27. In just a couple of weeks he would be in Indiana, a trip he had been eagerly anticipating all year but at the moment seemed like just a frivolous detail. "OK, moron, snap out of it and get to work," he finally said and started into his routine. CNN, ESPN, MSN, then messages. There were three, one of them for an assignment on the continued popularity of rodeos in California, one for coverage of a computer trade show in Las Vegas for a German trade magazine and one from Bea.

Bea. Phillips was supposed to meet her for coffee yesterday afternoon and had totally forgotten after leaving the doctor's office.

"Hey, Dick, missed you this afternoon. Everything all right? Love you, BT"

He made a mental note to call her today, maybe catch her for a meal tonight. "But no way am I going to tell her what is happening to me."

He read over the offer from the German magazine.

> Dear Mr. Phillips:
>
> Sorry this is such short notice, but our U.S. correspondent has taken ill and cannot attend this coming weekend's computer trade show in Las Vegas. We can pay you $1,000 plus expenses for weekend attendance and a 3,000-word article.
>
> Regards,
> Gunther Hobst,
>
> Technology Assigning Editor

"Not bad," Phillips thought. "A thousand bucks for a weekend of work." He loved doing work for overseas publications since they always paid well. Phillips wrote back:

Dear Mr. Hobst:

I'll be there. My address and Social Security number are included on my Web site, phillipsandman.com.

Cheers,
Tom Phillips

The week was taking shape, which in normal times would have pleased Phillips no end. A creature of habit, he loved routine, order and making plans. Order meant life was full, and a full life was a happy life. Did that make Phillips special or just one of the crowd? Who knows? And did the answer matter?

Phillips still had a couple of hours before his doctor's appointment, so he took a nap, then had a lunch of homemade chili with oyster crackers and a can of root beer, and took a shower. Whether he was going on a date or going to the grocery, Phillips always made a point of looking neat. He would never appear on the cover of GQ, but he would never be mistaken for someone homeless either.

Wearing a blue Polo shirt, jeans neatly pressed to give a good crease and brown loafers, Phillips walked into the doctor's office to hear what the rest of his life had in store for him.

The receptionist greeted him warmly. "Hi, Tom, good to see you. Doctor Frank will be with you shortly." As he turned to take a seat, an elderly couple walked out of the hallway from one of the examination rooms holding hands and stopped at the receptionist's desk. The man limped slightly. "We got the prescription and will call in a couple of weeks for another appointment," the woman said. Phillips watched them leave and smiled when he noticed their wedding rings, simple gold bands imbedded in the skin of gnarled hands. The husband held open the door for his wife, who turned to kiss him and tenderly said, "I love you." Then they were gone.

Phillips was thinking about the couple when a young boy interrupted him. "Hey, mister, look at this." The boy looked to be about 5 and was holding a sea shell.

"Jimmy, don't bother the man," said a woman sitting nearby. "Come back here and sit with me."

"No, that's OK, ma'am," Phillips replied. "I just think he's excited about this shell and wants to show someone." Like most single men, Phillips liked kids as long as they were someone else's. All except for Natalie, his sweet Natalie, now 24 and living in Chicago. The product of one night of carelessness during sex, she who had caused such fear in him before being born had turned out to be the love of his life and more precious than anything he could have ever imagined.

"I can't wait to see her again," Phillips said as he looked at the shell. "Huh?" the boy asked. "Oh, nothing, I was just thinking about my daughter and how I miss her."

"Mr. Phillips, the doctor will see you now," the receptionist interrupted.

"Good to meet you, is it Jimmy? Maybe we'll see each other again." The boy walked over to his mother as Phillips went up the hallway. Doctor Frank was waiting for him. "Hi, doctor, nice seeing you again."

"Hi, Tom. Let's go into my office and talk."

"That Jimmy seems nice," Phillips said. The doctor closed the door behind them and answered, "Yes, he's very nice, and very brave. He's a very sick boy."

Phillips stopped. "Oh?"

"Nobody ever said life was fair. I see it every day. Some people, like that elderly couple who just left, live into their 70s and 80s. They have had a good life, been coming to me along with their kids for about 30 years now. Then this boy may never see age 10. Don't try to explain it because there is no explanation."

Dr. Byron Frank, who could have walked straight out of Gone *With the Wind* with his genteel Southern manner, had been Phillips' doctor for 10 years, but until this came along the most serious thing he had ever had to see him for was a rabies shot when a stray cat bit him on the hand. He was relying on him now to be honest on what lay ahead.

Phillips looked at the wall for a few seconds, then said, "Doctor Frank, what exactly can I expect to happen to me?"

Byron Frank had counseled hundreds of ill or dying patients in his 35 years of practice, but one thing he had learned a long time ago was that each was unique in temperament and ability to handle the facts. Phillips had always impressed him as a straightforward man who wanted to cut to the chase, so that is just what the doctor did.

"Well, Tom, I won't get into all the medical details, but to put it simply, Alzheimer's is a brain disorder in which nerve cells die at a fast pace. This affects your memory but also eventually impacts vision and speech. It also will affect your emotions, can lead to depression and disorientation, and in its final stages basically robs you of your ability to take care of yourself.

"Up to you now you have only experienced the very earliest stage of the disease, and indeed while it's not common to develop the symptoms at your age it can hit people in their 30s."

Phillips listened and said nothing.

"I can direct you to literature and to Internet sites that will give you greater detail. In the meantime, realize you are not alone in this. I am here to help you, millions of other Americans are diagnosed with Alzheimer's, there are support groups, centers for those in the severe stages of it and constant research on ways to correct or minimize the effects of the disease. Already there is medicine available that in some cases can treat the symptoms of mild or moderate levels.

"And be aware there are counselors who can help you deal with this even in the early stages. May I ask, do you go to church or know of a priest or reverend you could talk to? Depression is a very real danger as time goes on and the Alzheimer's progresses."

For someone who prided himself on being level-headed and seemingly in control of his life and events, Phillips wasn't taking this well.

"I just don't know, Doctor Frank. I have to think about this."

He got up abruptly and turned to leave. "Tom, are you all right?" the doctor asked.

"I don't know, I just don't know. I'll make another appointment to talk more about this and and get that literature you talked about, OK?"

"As you wish, Tom. But please stay in touch with my office. We've got to make plans on treatment and your continuing awareness of the disease's effect on you."

"I can still go about my normal routine, can't I?"

"Of course, just be aware you may have memory lapses and mood changes for now."

"I won't die soon will I?"

"Life expectancy stretches into a number of years for Alzheimer's patients, and particularly one stricken in his late 40s like yourself. So don't go out of here fearing you will die in a few months or that you will suddenly find yourself in a neighborhood and not know where you are. This disease is degenerative, it takes time to reach its height. That in some ways is good, and in others is very bad."

"How do you mean, doctor?"

"You know what will eventually happen to you."

Tom shook the doctor's hand and opened the door to leave. "Tom?"

"Yes?"

"Do you keep a diary or journal?"

"What do you mean?"

"For many, many years I have kept a diary of my thoughts. I have always found it to be a wonderful means of dealing with my emotions during times of crisis or difficulty when I needed to think clearly."

"I have always been able to think about things better when I write them down," Phillips answered, remembering his note taking at the computer the night before. "You may have something. Thank you."

Phillips walked quickly out of the office, saying a "thank you" to the receptionist on the way. He stopped outside the building, leaned against the door and took in a deep breath. Phillips was thinking of a woman, Dorothy Schmidt, an Alzheimer's patient who stayed at the same nursing home as his dad. Whenever he visited his dad he passed her room and often wondered why she would just lay in bed and repeat her name over and over endlessly. Finally one day he asked a nurse why she did so and the nurse replied that maybe "She does it so she will remember her name."

"I wonder," Phillips said to the empty passenger seat as he started his car to go home, "if maybe she says her name because she wants to forget it."

CHAPTER 5

▼

BEA

The phone was ringing as Phillips turned the key in the lock. He pushed the door open, hurried in and grabbed the receiver. "Hey, Dick, how are you doing? I'm glad I caught you at home. Whatcha doing tonight?"

It was Bea. "Hey, BT, I was going to call you later. Sorry I missed you last night."

"Hey, no problem. I figure you were out chasing some high school skirt."

If anyone could cheer up Phillips, it was his friend Bea. A mite of a woman who took shit from no one, she was a researcher at the Library of Congress by day, a connoisseur of fine foods, sports nut and carouser by night.

"How about dinner later? There's a French place I've been dying to try, and I hoped you might want to go along," she said.

Phillips hesitated. Normally he would always be willing to take her up on an invitation, especially to a French restaurant, but the visit to the doctor's office had, at least for the moment, taken both his spirit and appetite.

"Is everything all right?" Bea finally said, sensing something was wrong.
"No, everything's fine." He wasn't convincing. "Sure, let's do it.
"Where?"
"You're sure? OK, it's Chez Panisse, in Dupont Circle, on Connecticut Avenue near R Street. Meet you there at 8."
"I know the place. Done."
"See ya. I have to get back to work now."
"Bye."

Phillips loved Bea. He wondered from time to time if they could have had a romance were she not gay, but he always ended up dismissing the thoughts as didn't matter, which they didn't. What mattered is that each loved and respected the other for what they were and how they lived, and anything beyond that were meaningless details.

Phillips was glad he would see her tonight. Even if he didn't tell her about the Alzheimer's, which he was determined not to do, just being with her would settle him down. "Besides, I'll be at the club anyway, and that's just a couple of blocks away," he told himself.

As the plans took shape, Phillips felt better. He had enough to keep him busy the rest of the week before leaving for Vegas, and then it would be less than a week before he began his drive back to Indiana.

"Maybe I can beat this after all." He thought again about Doctor Frank's idea of keeping a diary, went to his desk and took out another small notebook like the one he had started keeping phone numbers in. He opened the notebook, closed it, went to the refrigerator to get a bottle of beer and a meat loaf sandwich he had made that morning for an afternoon snack, then sat in his recliner thinking of Bea and the first time they had met. He smiled.

It was 1995. Phillips was sitting in the Metroliner ready to travel to New York, where he was to meet with the publisher of his novel, and was feeling good about things as he looked out the window of the train as it prepared to leave Union Station in Washington. A voice interrupted him.

"Excuse me, is this seat taken?"

He liked Bea from that first moment. She was cute, about 5 foot 1 and probably not much more than 100 pounds dripping wet. With tightly cropped blonde hair and engaging blue eyes, she instantly attracted Phillips.

"Sure, it's all yours," he answered immediately.

"Going to New York?"

"Yes, I'm meeting with a book publisher. How about you?"

"I'm going to New York to see a friend and a couple plays and have some good food."

Phillips wondered why of all the seats available on the train Bea had asked to sit next to him. She would later tell him that she felt comfortable seeing him there, though both would have found that hard to believe for the first hour of their ride together.

"So, you're a writer?"

"Yes, my first novel. I surprised even myself when a publisher in New York was interested in it."

"Why?"

"I wrote it almost on a lark. I'm a travel writer and wanted to see if I could write a book. I worked off and on for six months on a novel, sent it off to a couple of places and lo and behold, one of them wrote back and said they wanted to see me."

"What's it about?"

"It's titled *The Awakening*, a romance set in Mazatlan, Mexico, involving a jilted 26-year-old black woman from the Bronx who falls in love with a 59-year-old widower from Mississippi."

Bea looked at Phillips and laughed. "That sounds pretty stupid."

Phillips wasn't amused. "Well it may be, but the publisher I am going to meet doesn't seem to think so."

"What does it publish? Mad magazine?"

"Very funny. Say, what is your name? Or are you too busy being a smartass to tell me?"

"You yourself said you were surprised the publisher got back to you."

"Yeah, but not because the book was something out of Mad magazine. I just figured it was hard to break into the publishing business. Is your old man Ernest Hemingway?"

"OK, OK, I'm sorry. Let's start over. Maybe I should introduce myself. My name is Bea A. Farmer, and I work for the Library of Congress as a researcher. And you?"

Phillips laughed. "Your name is Bea A. Farmer, like be a farmer? I'll bet you took a lot of guff in school for that."

"School, job applications, you name it. When I would introduce myself in groups, I'd often get scolded for being a smart-aleck when I said my name. But that's what it is. First name is Bea, too, not Beatrice."

"And your middle name?"

"Agatha. My folks are huge Agatha Christie fans, and they told me it was either Agatha or Christie for my middle name. Christie seemed like too much of a mouthful, so Agatha it is. Too bad you didn't write a mystery. My parents would love you."

Phillips had to believe, even five years later, that Bea had never read his book, despite the wide success it would have, because he had written it under a pen name and she never once mentioned it to him.

As the train began its journey on that pleasant spring day, Phillips and Bea continued the conversation that would form the foundation of their friendship until, Phillips was certain, one or the other of them died.

"How about dinner sometime?"

"You're certainly direct."

"We writers of silly novels have to be."

"Well, I'll be direct too, then. We can have dinner sometime if you like, but I will tell you from the start that I am gay."

Phillips was startled, and Bea noticed it.

"Why does that surprise you?"

"You're so pretty."

Bea snorted. "Being pretty means you HAVE to like men?"

"No, I just always assumed."

"You assumed wrong. Why am I sitting here anyway?"

"No one's forcing you."

Bea didn't move.

Phillips turned to look at the other passengers near them and see if they were listening to their conversation. All appeared to be absorbed in conversations of their own, reading, on cell phone calls or sleeping. The train clicked along the tracks.

"So," he finally said, "do you ever dip?"

"What do you mean dip?"

"Ever have a man just for a change?"

"You know, men are weird by nature, but you really are one crazy bugger."

"Well?"

"Yes, I do sometimes, but only with men of color. Why am I telling you this?"

"Men of color?" Phillips raised an eyebrow.

"Yes, white men have too many hangups."

"I'll bet I know why."

"Do tell."

"Because you think men of color have bigger dicks. What's this nonsense about white men having hangups?"

"I think you're answering your own question."

Phillips thought on that point for a moment and looked out the window. He loved this ride, loved the feeling of freedom that the rails gave him. And now here he was making a total idiot of himself with a woman who asked nothing more than whether she could sit next to him and chat for a few hours.

"And let me tell you one thing. Size doesn't really matter after all."

"Oh?"

"Let me ask you. Do you think a woman has to have big tits to give good sex?"

"Of course not." Phillips looked at Bea. She had a slight figure but was, by his immediate reckoning, probably dynamite in bed.

"Well then?"

"So I'll back off. But do me a favor."

"Maybe."

"Don't talk about people of color because it's wrong."

"Why?"

"Isn't white a color?"

"Of course."

"Then you can't say people of color as a means of distinguishing them from people who are white."

Bea extended her hand. "Deal. You quit talking about dicks and tits and all those other sillyass ideas you have in your white head, and I'll quit talking about color."

"Sold."

"What travel articles do you write for a living? Or do you just go around on trains making ridiculous remarks to women?"

For the rest of the trip, Bea and Phillips told each other about themselves, their hobbies, their work, their lives, their hopes and their failings. When the train pulled into Penn Station in New York City, they had made plans for dinner and a movie. The seed of their friendship was planted on that day, and it had grown and blossomed in the years since.

Phillips sat back in the recliner and replayed that first meeting with Bea. They still laughed about it from time to time, felt as comfortable with each other as any two people could, or at least he had thought so. His smile faded as he realized that he could not or would not confide in her about this turn in his life.

The meat loaf sandwich half-eaten, Phillips returned to the notebook and began to write.

CHAPTER 6

▼

THE DIARY

Tuesday, June 27

I feel like a stranger. I am starting this diary because Doctor Frank said it would be a good idea. Is it? Who knows. Maybe it doesn't matter. What a lot of bullshit that is, me and my doesn't matter crap. Maybe I've always thought things didn't matter because I didn't take them seriously or I was just too stupid or too shallow to realize that they did. Anyway what difference does it make? In 10 or 15 years I won't be able to remember my own name or be able to take a leak without someone to help me since I will have forgotten where my fly is. I wonder if I'll forget where my dick is. Funny how easy it always was to visit Dad in the nursing home and go around and try to cheer up the other inmates. I wonder if all along they have hated me and told themselves how easy it was for me to say cheer up when I was able to go home and they were stuck there forever. There's just no way I'm going to stick around for the next dozen years hoping some miracle cure comes up. What if it doesn't? What then? I'll end

up like them, too gone to do anything about, and there's no way I'm going to hang around friends or family hoping they take in the invalid Tom.
SON OF A BITCH!!!

Phillips read over his diary notes. "Well, that went swell. I wonder if Doctor Frank realized what he was getting me into with this. I sound like a fuckin' madman." He thought of just chucking the thing into the garbage can, but instead stayed motionless in thought for a few seconds, folded the cover and put the notebook into his desk drawer.

The phone rang. Phillips was going to let the answering machine kick in, then lunged for the receiver on the fifth ring to catch the caller in time. "Hi, Tommy. How's my little sandman?"

"Hi, Mom. I'm fine. I was just thinking about you." Phillips said that whether he was thinking of her or not. He often wondered whether she believed him or minded that his opening was always the same, but then she always wondered if her adult son minded being called Tommy and her little sandman, pet names from his childhood a long time ago

"How's Dad doing?"

"He's well, as always. I'm going to visit him in an hour and wanted to make sure your trip here next month was still on so I could tell him. You know how he always loves seeing you."

"Yes, Mom, I'll definitely be there in July. I'm looking forward to it." That was something he always did mean. Phillips loved going back to his hometown to see his parents, whom he deeply loved and respected. Joe and Peggy. Two people as solid and unpretentious as their names. In an age when divorce, which to Phillips was nothing more than the destruction or failure of a relationship, was accepted and indeed celebrated by some, his parents had maintained a stable, loving relationship for 49 years. If they fought, he and Kate had never heard it, and while they surely had disagreements from time to time, Phillips had never heard them descend into bickering or name-calling.

When they were younger, Phillips used to like teasing Kate about their parents having sex.

"Hey, Kate," the exchange usually went, "do you think Mom and Dad ever have kinky sex?"

"You're disgusting, you pig. Cut it out."

"No, I mean it, how do you think Dad arouses Mom?"

"Tom, no more."

"Do you think Dad ever …"

Kate stuck her fingers in her ears. "I won't listen."

"…got Mom on the floor…"

"La-la-la-la-la, I'm not listening to this," Kate yelled as she ran from the room.

Phillips got a kick out of those exchanges and still laughed about them even though he hadn't teased Kate about it for more than 30 years. Though Kate might disagree, he considered such antics part of a healthy attitude toward his parents, one built on humor, maturity and love. In Phillips' most private conversations with himself, he believed that, strangely enough, one reason he had never married was that he was afraid his own might not live up to that of his parents'. He had never told anyone but would believe to his dying day that that was the reason he had refused to marry Helena.

"Does Dad need anything?" Phillips liked bringing trinkets from Washington back to his dad, who put them on his dresser in the nursing home.

"No, he has everything he needs. Just come back to him for that visit soon. I will see him today and remind him that you are visiting."

"OK, I'll call again soon. I love you and tell Dad I love him."

"Bye, Tommy. I love you."

Joe had been in the nursing home a little over two years, and not one day in that time had Peggy failed to visit him. She would never have put him there in the first place, but as Joe got older and needed help dressing, eating and bathing, Peggy was unable to care for him properly. So every day, rain, snow or shine, she would board the bus and visit her husband, sit with him during lunch and sometimes dinner as well, watch television with him, and spend their last years devoted to him, as she had their first 49.

His dad was 76 now, his mom 78. "Your mother always did like younger men," Joe would joke with his only son. A construction worker until he turned 65, Joe had lived a life filled with hard work and the joy of creating things with his hands. He built homes and could fix just about anything around a house, mostly because he could visualize how something was put together or should be put together. Phillips, on the other hand, couldn't nail two pieces of wood together without ruining one of them, but it didn't matter because he could construct something else, thanks to his mother, a librarian who had taught him a love of books and the power of the written word. Phillips could construct sentences into paragraphs, paragraphs into pages and pages into stories and chapters. He had built a fulfilling life as a writer.

While his parents had been content to never travel far from their home outside South Bend, Tom loved seeing America and the world and by now had been to 40 states, along with South America, Europe and Asia. His mom and dad had always insisted on seeing his travel articles, and he dutifully always mailed them a copy.

One thing he had never told them about was his book. To keep it a secret he had written it under the pen name Philip Sandman. "Why in the world won't you tell them?" Bea had asked him when he told her why he hadn't used his real name as author of *The Awakening*. "I'm sure they would be proud of you."

"I'm just not taking that chance. Parts of it are too racy for them." And while indeed his book had included any number of provocative sex scenes plus a whole lot of foul language, there was no way he could prove his mom and dad would have objected. "For that matter, they may even like it," argued Kate when he told her. Phillips would laugh. "Aren't you the liberal thinker, Miss La-La-La, who used to plug her ears when I teased you about their sex life."

"I'm not so sure they are the same thing," Kate answered. But there the conversation had ended, and nothing Phillips had heard or did since then had convinced him to own up to his book.

For sure, his dad would have been especially proud of the money he had made from it. Phillips had written *The Awakening* just to see if he had the stamina and imagination to keep a cohesive story going for 200 pages. When he had sent it off to publishers he had never expected to get anything more than rejection letters, which he did get a lot of. But then one day he got the letter from a small publisher in New York, and it was on that train ride that he had met Bea. "Two lucky strokes from one train trip," he would tell himself later.

Phillips signed a contract for the book, which ended up on best-seller lists for more than six months. In the first two years he made over $400,000 in after-tax royalties, and then made it even better by investing in the go-go stock market to nearly triple his money. He put the $1.2 million in Treasury bonds paying 6 percent, giving him interest of more than $70,000 a year. Coupled with earnings from freelance articles and a part-time job as a dishwasher that he still kept because he liked the physical nature of the work, Phillips was bringing home $105,000 a year, more than enough for all of his needs and his pleasures.

While Joe and Peggy never did know how much exactly their son made from that book, or that he had been as astute as his dad in parlaying his earnings into a nice fortune from the stock market, they had known from the very beginning he had written it. The style and nuance were ones that only could have come from their son. And if that weren't enough, the author's name was a dead giveaway. "Philip Sandman. Really," Peggy said to Joe after they had bought a copy. "Did he really think he could fool us? If he did, he should never have picked the name Sandman," she said. Peggy smiled, just as she always had when singing the "Sandman song" as Tom had called it as a boy when his mom sang it to him, a popular tune from the 1950s. While she hadn't heard it on the radio in many years, Peggy continued to sing her variation of it when she was happy and thinking about her boy and all he meant to her life.

Both Peggy and Joe had read *The Awakening* cover to cover and loved every word of it, even the sex scenes, which they found titillating and not altogether foreign.

Phillips was about to sign on to his computer when the phone rang again. "Hi, Tom, it's Helena. Are you coming to the club tonight?"

"Sure thing, Helena. I hope to see you there because I am going out of town next week on a trip back to Indiana. I had been wanting to see you before I go."

"Good. Thomas and I will look for you there, say about 6?"

"I'll be there. Love you. Bye."

"Till then. Love you."

Phillips went back to his PC and found a message from Doctor Frank giving him some Web sites for checking out the symptoms and treatment of Alzheimer's, along with sources for support groups and counseling if needed.

He called up one and read through it. It was much like what Doctor Frank had described. Memory loss of recent events and names in the first stages, not being able to find things, getting lost. Then worsening loss of memory, bouts of anxiety and depression and finally requiring care from others, more mental disintegration, inability to recognize family members. "In other words, I become almost like a vegetable, and worse yet, as the years go on I know this will happen to me. At least with a heart attack it just hits and kills me." Phillips angrily clicked off the Web site and shut down his computer, went into his desk and took out the notebook again.

Later Tuesday, June 27

Here I am again. I can't understand why I feel so weak about this when the other people in my life seem so strong. Would Mom and Dad be acting this way? Would Helena? Bea? Kate? Could it be that I am afraid of being dependent on someone else, or maybe I am ashamed to be? Why am I asking all of these questions when Doctor Frank laid out what will happen and how I can get help? Death has never scared me before, but maybe it's because I never had to seriously think about it. Funny how we think we can handle these things when we're just playing and then when they look us right in the eye we shit our pants out of fear or indecision. I don't know what to do, but then maybe I really do and just don't want to admit it.

It was getting late. Phillips read over his notes, even began warming to the diary almost as talking to a secret friend and put away the notebook. Evening approached and his friends would be at the club.

Alzheimer's could wait, if only for the night.

CHAPTER 7

HELENA

The club was nothing to look at. A run-down bar and grill by the standards of chic, upscale Dupont Circle, it attracted a crowd that snubbed its nose at the image-conscious power brokers and wannabes of Washington. In other words, it was a perfect hangout for Phillips. He could go there for company, food, drinking and females, in no particular order. In fact, it was at the club that Phillips had set a goal for himself to bed women from as many races, nationalities and religions as he could. He called them his food groups. After all, a man's gotta eat.

Phillips would never rank among the best lovers of the world, either in terms of performance or number of conquests. But he was a modest man by nature so it was the goal, the idea, the plan that counted as much as anything. His favorites thus far were the Japanese woman Nobuku he had met in the beer line at a Red Sox game in Boston, the Indian Swariddi he had chatted up over a plate of curry in Chicago while both were attending a books trade show and the German Gretel who had insisted on tying him up and reading Goethe in a hotel in Los Angeles. For some time now he had wanted to add a Jewish woman to the list and tonight he hoped to nail this one down as well. Her name was Paula Rosenthal, a slightly built woman with auburn hair, thin lips, a cute smile and whom Phillips imagined whimpering ever so delicately as he entered her.

The club's real name was Bennys' Club, named for a grizzled old fart named – you guessed it – Benny, and his son named – take another wild guess – Benny Junior. Benny did this more as a hobby now than anything else. He had started the place back in the 1960s and named it Benny's. Over the years he had invested his modest income wisely in mutual funds. Thirty-some years of steady investment in the stock market had done wonders for his bank account so that by now he was worth well over a million bucks. His wife had died some years before, and Benny had little else to do but tend to the club, so he was a popular fixture with Phillips and his crowd. He had changed the name to the plural Bennys' after his son, deciding his master's degree in English literature would never get him anywhere, asked his dad if he needed help running the place. And thus a partnership was born.

One thing the old man did well other than invest wisely was to make just about the best hamburger on the planet, at least in the humble opinion of Phillips. And tonight, even though he had eaten a sandwich not two hours before and would have a fine dinner with Bea just two hours hence, he needed a Benny special. Not only would it help him eat away his cares, the meat surely would strengthen him for what he hoped would be a good romp with Paula. Phillips went immediately to the bar as he entered the club, found Benny and ordered.

"Hi, Benny. How are things?"

"Tom, haven't seen you in a couple of days. You been OK?"

"Yeah, just hanging around home and enjoying the summer. Hey, Benny, I need one of your specials. Medium well, fried onions, butter on the bun, an inch of pickles, spicy mustard. Got it?"

"Yeah, the usual. Coming right up."

Benny retreated to the kitchen, and Junior took over the bar duties.

It was still early in the evening, and most of the crowd hadn't come in yet. Phillips was eager to see Bea and Helena tonight, and Paula hadn't come by yet either. So for now, it would be him and that glorious burger.

Just then Doug Bledso walked in. Twenty pounds overweight with a bowl haircut and fuhrer mustache, he pissed off Phillips just by entering the room. Bledso was a wordsmith for one of the D.C. newspapers and was everything Phillips hated about editors: A self-assured, unctuous perfectionist who thought he walked on water because he could conjugate the verb lay. Of course, Phillips assured himself, getting laid was seldom in Bledso's vocabulary.

Bledso walked up to Phillips uninvited. "So, Phillips, how's every little thing?"

"Swell, Doug, how about you?"

"Everything's great. Ever wish you worked at a newspaper, Mr. Travel Writer?"

This was a common question from Bledso, intended every time as a suggestion that Phillips was somehow the citizen of a lower kingdom because he didn't work with the world's ink jockeys.

"Yeah, I wish for it, Bledso, about as much as your ex-girlfriends wish they still were with you."

"My, my, touchy, touchy. What crawled up your ass, Phillips?"

"You did, Bledso, and both of you smell about the same."

Phillips actually hated the news business mainly because he hated the news. For someone who once had dreams of being a politician, Phillips made an amazing turnabout. He thought the Congress was full of hot air and couldn't stand just about any politician you could name. News coverage of Washington to him was nothing more than a bunch of ill-dressed reporters who were power wannabes. More, the world was a shithole run by assholes, where people killed each other over land and sports jackets and yet a doctor who wanted to help put dying people out of their misery was himself hounded by the authorities.

Bledso took another slug of his beer and looked at Phillips. "Say, how's your dike friend?" About the only thing that irritated Phillips more about Bledso than his insufferable air of perfection and cocksuredness that he knew everything about everything was his failing that all supposedly open-minded people had. They were open-minded so long as you agreed with them, and once you dared cross swords with their hallowed opinion you were nothing more than a lowlife.

And it turns out that Bledso hated gays. Bledso and Bea had detested each other at first sight, and their relationship went downhill from there.

"Funny you should ask, Doug. Just the other day she asked about you."

"She did?" Bledso's eyebrows raised.

"Yeah, she asked me, 'Do you still go out drinking with that piece of shit Dug-LASS?"

"Real funny, Phillips. Too bad I'll miss seeing her and her muff-diver friends tonight. I'm off to work." Bledso drained the remainder of his beer.

"Give those semicolons hell, Doug," Phillips yelled after him.

Bledso gave him the finger and walked out the door.

As Bledso left, the hamburger arrived, proving to Phillips there is a God. He took the plate and retreated to a rear table. As Phillips sat there savoring each bite of the sandwich, done just right as always, he reflected on the Bledsos of the world. "Why do assholes like that get to keep on going and I end up with Alzheimer's?" All he knew that Bledso suffered from was assholishness and his disgusting haughtiness, but neither would kill him or rob him of his ability to function as an adult.

There was but one thing Phillips and Bledso ever agreed on, and that was their distaste for the dot-com crowd, the dot-comers as they liked to call them, who thought they were slumming it by going to the club. Every last one was a self-important little twit who strutted around and bragged about being on the leading edge. "Wouldn't it be poetic justice," Phillips and Bledso would take turns saying to each other when they spotted a bunch of them, "if the dot-coms crashed someday and these jerks would have to go around looking for jobs?"

As Phillips took the last bite of his hamburger and washed it down with a nice swallow of draft beer, Helena walked in. If there was such a thing as heaven on Earth, it was Helena Zimmer. And the funny, and sad, thing was that Phillips had had a chance to make her his very own and walked away.

"Helena," Phillips called to her as she walked in with her husband and they looked over the crowd for familiar faces. "Hi, Tom," Helena said affectionately. Phillips rose to hug her and kiss her gently on the check, then reached past her to shake hands with her husband, Thomas, and said to him, "Always good to see you."

"Tom, likewise," Helena's husband said and went to get a beer for himself and glass of wine for Helena. He knew she always wanted a moment with Phillips for herself. Thomas was aware that his wife had not totally lost her love for Phillips, but he accepted it. Thomas and Helena had two children together and a wonderful life, and he wasn't about to begrudge his wife, whom he loved dearly, the remnants of affection for a man in her past.

"How's my sandman?" Helena asked. She was one of the few close to Phillips whom he had told about his book as its popularity grew.

"I'm doing fine. You look great, as always."

"How's Natalie?"

"She's well. I'm seeing her next month when I travel back to Indiana."

"That's right. Please remember me to your parents."

"I will."

Phillips' parents had never quite forgiven him for letting Helena get away, and both they and she continued to stay in touch and retain affection from afar. In fact, it was impossible for anyone not to like Helena Zimmer. She radiated charm, had a laugh like the tinkling of a wind chime blowing gently in the breeze and took life as it was meant to be taken – on its own terms and accepting its beauty without being burdened with its ugliness. It was perhaps her eyes that were the most captivating, certainly for the men who admired her, of which there were many. "The eyes are the windows to the soul," Helena had once told Phillips. At the time he had blown it off as just bullshit, but after getting to know her after loving her, he realized how right she had been. Phillips had never seriously regretted having not stayed with Helena, yet her absence from his life left him with a feeling of emptiness deep inside, especially late at night when there was only the stillness to remind him of what he had once had and then lost.

The only time Phillips had ever been jealous was when she said of Thomas, "He completes me." He could think of no thing more wonderful for one person to say about another.

Thomas came over to her now with his beer and her wine. "Coming to our place for dinner tomorrow, Tom?" Helena asked. Phillips had totally forgotten about the invitation extended a week ago. He hesitated, then said, "Of course."

"You don't sound so sure. We can make it another time if you want, but I do have your birthday card for you, though it's early."

"No, I'll be there."

Thomas took a drink of his beer and looked over the crowd. It was the usual. A few dot-comers vastly outnumbered by the newspaper people and others who lived on the fringes of Washington respectability. Thomas and Helena were probably the only two people there who were out of their element. He was a lawyer at the Federal Communications Commission and she a staff aide at the Justice Department. They had a home in Maryland, entertained and attended dinner and cocktail parties with the mainstream of Washington politics and bureaucracy and generally played by all the rules of D.C. society. Sometimes Phillips wondered why Helena had even been interested in him in light of the life she had built with Thomas. He and Thomas were worlds apart in almost every way but one, and that was their mutual love for Helena. Still, Thomas genuinely liked Phillips. Part of that was simply because his wife cared for Phillips. But he also saw in

Phillips a part of himself that he kept hidden away from his starched-shirt world. He admired Phillips' pride in individuality, in being true to a simple lifestyle and mindset, in Phillips demand of himself that he live by his own rules. Thomas knew nothing of Phillips' financial and artistic success as an author but nevertheless sometimes wistfully talked of his ability to make a living without having to slavishly tow the Washington line as he himself had to do.

Phillips caught Thomas looking at him. "So, Thomas, how are things at the FCC?"

"Oh, pretty much the usual, Tom, that is to say actually quite hectic. I'm involved these days with the direction of cable TV, which is just part of the communications revolution sweeping America."

Thomas stopped himself, realizing he was talking like he was at a cocktail party with a bunch of stiff-necks. "You know, Tom, it's really the same old shit. Say, you seeing anybody these days?"

Helena smiled.

"What's so funny, love?" Thomas asked his wife.

"Oh, your question just reminded me of what Tom told me long ago about the three kinds of women he never dated."

"And they are?"

"Drug users, anyone who broke up with a boyfriend within the last year and liberals."

"Liberals?" Thomas chuckled. "Why liberals?"

Phillips smiled and took a drink of his beer. "Because sooner or later they always have issues."

Thomas had to laugh at that himself. "I'll remember that the next time I'm at a party where some of these insufferable Washington types are full of themselves."

Just then Rodger Reed walked into the bar, saw Phillips, Thomas and Helena and walked to them.

"How are you folks tonight?" he asked.

The two men said "Fine" at the same time. Helena walked to Reed as he approached, hugged him and kissed him gently on the check and said, "Always good to see you, Rodger."

"Likewise, Helena."

Reed was a sophisticated man. He covered the State Department for the Washington Post, had traveled widely, loved good food the world over and dressed so smartly no one would ever think at first glance that he worked at a newspaper. He had piercing blue eyes, coiffed light brown hair and a charming Southern accent with a voice so low that when he talked his words seem to reach from the pit of his stomach. Phillips, Thomas and Helena always loved having him around for his wit, tales of travel and generally wise views of the world.

All three sensed something was on his mind tonight, and they were right.

Helena spoke. "Is everything all right, Rodger? You seem tense."

Reed ordered a glass of Chablis and a double plate of buffalo wings. He may have enjoyed fine cuisine, but he also knew good nosh when he saw it. "I talked to my dad this afternoon and his mom has taken a severe turn for the worse with her cancer. My grandmother was a vibrant woman, a banker and an artist, and now she is reduced to wearing diapers and basically waiting to die."

"We're all sorry to hear that," Thomas said. Phillips listened.

"I know we've talked philosophically before about the right to die, in this very establishment, but never more than now has that right seemed so painfully evident and indeed correct," Reed said. "And yet, the government would deem me or my father a killer if we were to put that good woman out of her misery. She herself would welcome it.

"We make a huge issue in this country of the right to life. Where are the crowds when it comes to the right to die?" Reed was angry, his features hard. He took a sip of his wine and continued.

"We send someone like Jack Kevorkian to jail when we should be using him as a model. God dammit!" He pounded his fist on the bar so hard patrons within 10 feet stopped talking and turned to look at him.

Phillips had never seen Reed, normally a careful and disciplined man, in such a state. He was intrigued by Reed's arguments. And he agreed with them. Phillips in fact had written a term paper for a college psychology class discussing this very topic. He had forgotten all about it until this moment.

Reed went to the bar to collect his order of buffalo wings, then motioned the others to join him at a nearby table. As they all sat down and each started chewing, the conversation resumed.

"Just when do people have the right to die and does anyone else have the right to make that decision for them?" Reed asked in a question directed more to himself than anyone else. "You're on very shaky medical, legal and moral ground there, my friend," Thomas answered. "If you do anything to shorten the life of someone you are opening yourself for prosecution and perhaps jail, regardless of their suffering."

"Maybe," Phillips said. "But perhaps the punishment is worth the action if it shortens the suffering of someone you love."

Helena looked at him with surprise. "I've never heard you say such a thing, Tom," she said. "Do you really believe this?"

"Of course I do. The best course naturally is for the person suffering to make the decision himself or herself and to be the one who actually takes his or her own life. That way there are no consequences."

The three other people at the table looked at Phillips.

"So you believe someone is justified in committing suicide?" Reed asked.

"Without question," Phillips responded. "The thing to do is for the person to act while he or she still can. No one else is involved then, and it is painless for all concerned."

"Except for the person who dies," Helena said.

Phillips made a mental note to discuss this further in his diary writing tonight, then looked at his watch. "Sorry, folks," he said as he got up to leave. "It's 7:30 and I have to meet Bea at 8. Helena and Tom, see you tomorrow night, say 7?"

"Sounds good to me," Helena said. "So long," said Reed and Thomas.

As Phillips was leaving, he saw Paula at the bar. "Shit, I got so wrapped up in that discussion with Rodger I forgot all about her," he muttered. Phillips had intended to make time with her before dinner with Bea, then return to chat her up, take her to his place and bone her. Aside from the fact that he wasn't in the mood any longer and hadn't implemented the first part of his plan, the guy standing alongside her complicated matters. Making them even more complicated was the rock he saw on her ring finger as she reached out to shake his hand.

"Tom, I'd like you to meet my fiance, Michael." Phillips hadn't seen her in a couple of months, but it still came as a shock to see she had gotten engaged. "Tom, a pleasure," Michael said. "Have you two known each other long?"

"About a couple of years. Maybe we'll talk again sometime, Michael, but I've really got to run to dinner now," Phillips said and started toward the door.

"Hope so," Michael said. "See you, Tom," Paula added. As he turned away, Paula pulled him closer and whispered, "You stupid bastard, you waited too long."

C H A P T E R   8

▼

THE ANSWER

As he hurried to dinner with Bea, Phillips lamented the blown opportunity to get some Jewish snatch. Settling his car into a parking garage near the restaurant, he dismissed the pangs in his mind and crotch with a shrug. "She probably powdered it anyway and just would have made me sneeze."

Bea was waiting for him inside, punctual as always. She rose to meet Phillips as he walked to their table.

"Dick, I've missed you," she said as they hugged.

"BT, it has been a couple of weeks, hasn't it?"

For all those around them knew, these were two lovers who had been apart and were glad to be with each other again. They had the glow and warmth of people genuinely glad to be in each other's company, right down to the pleasantries that only a couple close to each other could know. Bea had been calling him Dick since about a week into their friendship when she teased him once in a voice message by saying, "Hey, Big Dick, how's about a drink tonight?" He had returned the favor by leaving her a message answering, "Big Tits, I'd love to." From there the names had been shortened to just Dick and BT, and while for Phillips it was a playful thing, for Bea it actually worked out in her own mindset. The last man she had been romantically involved with was named Tom, a brute who thought because she gave him her pussy he had the right to hit, curse and mistreat her. She had sworn off male lovers for years and even detested the name. So Dick it was, and when Phillips found out the reason, he embraced it, hugged her and whispered in her ear, "I wish I could hug all your pain away."

Bea and Phillips had some good things in common, and one of them was a taste for fine food, particularly French. Tonight she ordered escargots in garlic butter followed by boneless duck breast with demi glace, brandy and apricot. Phillips started with mushrooms sautéed in a garlic cream sauce stuffed in a puff pastry, then for the main course filet of free-range veal with demi glace, brandy and tarragon. Over dinner and a bottle of white wine, followed by a demitasse and cheesecake with strawberries, they caught up on life and their friendship.

"Things are well with you, BT?" Phillips asked.

"Very," she answered. They begin their typical discussion of all the political nonsense choking the city when Phillips decided that of all the people he was close to, Bea was the one he could confide in about his Alzheimer's, indeed the one he suddenly felt he wanted to confide in.

"BT, I've something to tell you. Now please just listen to me and don't ask me a lot of questions, okay?"

"Sure," she replied.

"I went to the doctor yesterday and he confirmed to me that I have the early stages of Alzheimer's. The symptoms are very mild at this point, but certainly I must think about how I will deal with this."

As soon as the words got out of his mouth Phillips wished he hadn't told her. Bea looked at him, put her face in her hands and started to cry. He was more startled by her reaction than he was about his own willingness to tell her.

"Why are you crying?" he asked.

"Why am I crying? Isn't that kind of a silly question?"

"Well, I was just confiding in you and letting you know something about my life. It's something I have to deal with, not you."

"Do you think I have no feelings whatsoever? How would you expect me to react when you tell me such a thing?"

Phillips hadn't imagined how Bea would react because he never considered she had any real feelings for him, at least nothing beyond the Platonic friend-to-friend relationship they had always had. He himself found thinking from time to time of how nice it might be to love Bea as a woman and she him as a man, but he immediately dismissed the thoughts as something that could never happen. He wouldn't commit, and she had no interest in men.

"Bea, I wasn't looking for pity when I told you."

"There is a difference between pity and caring, Tom," Bea said, calling him by his first name, and he by hers, for the first time in a very long time. "Do you pity your father when you visit him in the nursing home, or do you care for him?"

Phillips had no answer.

They sat in awkward silence for a few minutes, drinking their coffee and picking at their dessert.

"What is success to you, Tom?"

"What do you mean?"

"Do you think success is having money or traveling a lot or being independent? Or do you think it is having responsibilities? To me, no matter how much a person has done in their life, it is rubbish if in their obituary the last line reads, 'He left no survivors.'"

"I'm amazed to hear you say things like this, Bea. I always thought you were the independent one who went her own way and to hell with what the world thought."

"Maybe I am, or was. But with something like this, Tom, you need all the people around you can find."

"There are alternatives."

"Such as?"

"There just are."

"Have you told your parents?"

"Not yet. I am not sure when I will."

Bea just looked at him, now completely at a loss.

"I mean, what could they say? I don't want everyone to make a big frigging deal of this. It's my problem, and I will take care of it." Phillips thought of the conversation with Rodger.

"Tom, I would like to help you." Bea reached across the table to take Phillips' hand. He pulled away.

Bea got up. "Don't walk me out, Tom. I just want to go home and think about this and deal with it as best I can."

Phillips looked up at her. "Okay, but please don't tell anyone, I beg of you."

Bea left without answering.

"Dammit," Phillips said as he turned and watched her walk out the door.

Bea walked to her car. It was a pleasant summer evening. Couples strolled past, hand in hand, laughing and happy. Bea was finally realizing she wanted these things too, that her rebellion against men had gone far enough. She had even thought of telling Phillips tonight, or maybe telling him if she decided to surprise him by showing up at his parents' party back in Indiana next month. Now all that was gone, or at least changed forever.

"Damn him. This is what I get," she said.

Bea switched direction. Instead of going to her house, she decided to surprise her new lover, Ben Magnuson, a 62-year-old widower. Tall, urbane and a one-time minor league baseball player, Ben was a veteran congressional staffer who had made a good living hawking his administrative abilities on the staffs of members of Congress. He now worked for one of the senators from Alaska. Bea had met him at a Capitol Hill fund-raising cocktail party over a dinner of Alaskan king crab. She had been surprised at being taken aback by this man and was even more surprised when she agreed to go back to his apartment that night after the party.

They had been lovers for three months now and while she knew nothing ever permanent would come of it, she did enjoy his company. With his mane of gray hair that he slicked back for work each day, Bea had nicknamed him Big Gray, though never to his face.

"Ben, I've just got to talk," she said when he answered the door to his apartment. "Absolutely, come on in, Bea. Can I get you something to drink?"

"Sure, tea if you have it, please."

She and Ben sat up until 3 talking about Phillips, though she never identified him, and when she finally fell asleep sitting in Ben's big recliner in the living room, he went to get a blanket and gently covered her and kissed her goodnight on the cheek.

Phillips had remained at the restaurant, sipping coffee and thinking about the night's events. After paying the check, he drove home, slipped into a pair of comfortable boxer shorts, watched the ESPN highlights and tried to relax.

"Dammit, I shouldn't have told her. Not only did she carry on, but she may tell someone." Phillips couldn't stand the idea of being dependent, even on someone he was as close to as Bea.

"Maybe I ruined our relationship tonight," he said. "It doesn't really matter anymore." Phillips stared out the window, then poured himself a glass of orange soda from the refrigerator and sat down at the desk. He took out the notebook.

Tuesday night, June 27

Telling Bea about my Alzheimer's tonight was about the stupidest thing I could have done. I want to talk to somebody about this but she obviously was the wrong one. I think tomorrow afternoon I will go to church and maybe try to meet that priest, Father Luke, and set up lunch for sometime next week. Surely I can confide in a priest, can't I?

Was Bea right tonight in my confusing concern with pity? Maybe I am too independent. I know that is what kept me from being with Helena, and it stopped me from even raising the subject of romantic love with Bea. I can't stand this idea of waiting for something to just come get me in the vain hope there might be a cure or some half-assed band-aid remedy.

As Phillips tapped his pencil on the notebook and looked up at the ceiling in thought, it came to him.

He went into his walk-in closet and came out with a duffel bag. The gun was just where he had left it a month ago after some target practice. Phillips had applied for a permit a couple of years ago and once approved had bought a .357 magnum. He had never been assaulted or even threatened, but Phillips felt more secure having the gun around. Plus it made him feel a bit like being in the old West, a six-shooter there to protect him if need be. He had never shot in anger but tried to go at least once a month to a shooting range just to squeeze off a few rounds and somehow feel connected with the days of gunslingers and cowboys.

In his bedroom, he looked over the gun and smiled at it as the answer he might be looking for. "No more tears from Bea or, God forbid, my parents if they find out. No more fake pity or forced concern." Phillips' own bitterness or self-sufficiency run amok surprised even him enough to stop and really think about what he was saying and contemplating doing.

He went back to his notebook.

This is not a bad idea at all. The real question is when. Frankly I'd like to get this over with so I'm not hanging around and thinking about this day and night. He sat back in his chair and thought, then suddenly sat up as an idea exploded in his head. Phillips returned to the notebook.

Why not next month when I am back for the visit? It'll be quick, I don't have to wait around for this thing to come get me and frankly

*there'll be no better time for it. Shit, it's almost like it's pre-ordained.
Saturday the 15th? Who would have thought? Man, I never
thought it would come to this. God, can I really...?*

Phillips didn't want to think anymore or try to answer the questions
tonight. He stopped writing, closed the notebook and went to sleep. The
Bible sat on the nightstand, unopened.

C H A P T E R 9

▼

No Turning Back

The alarm clock read 3:19. Phillips had slept fitfully, and even worse heard noises. He staggered into the living room. "My gosh, the TV is still on. I forgot to shut the damn thing off."

He wasn't sure if he had left it on like this before. He couldn't recall doing so. And even if he had, was it going to be like this, habits and things he had done absent-mindedly in the past becoming more and more exaggerated, simple mistakes that he would have blown off magnified now as the beginning of the end for a forgetful old fool? When he got out of bed, he couldn't even remember where the light switch was.

"Well if this is the way it is to be I'd best prepare for it as long as I am still around," Phillips said. He got out his notebook and added to the list: check appliances. Switch is on the wall just to the left of the doorway. Remember to wipe after you take a crap. "I'll just have to go down this list every night to keep my electricity bill from going haywire or leaving on a burner or something and burning the place down and me with it or killing myself with my own stench." He got out a handful of Oreo cookies, a glass of milk and enjoyed the quiet of the early morning, for the moment putting his cares away. Cookies had a habit of doing that to him. "Maybe I'll have an Oreo before I pull the trigger. God, you're a crazy son of a bitch. I had such hopes for going gracefully into old age and enjoying every minute of it." Phillips loved talking to himself. Maybe that's why he never needed that much company, at least until now when the answers he was getting in his self-conversation weren't enough or were the wrong ones.

He sat there in the early-morning hours, stared at the wall and thought of Bea. He thought of how they cuddled while watching some silly Western on TV. She would kiss him on the neck and he on her nose. He thought of his fondness and affection for her, now turning into a wall since he had let her in on his secret. "What am I afraid of?" he asked in the stillness of his own mind. "Am I afraid of Bea? Death? Commitment? The end of my illusions?"

The darkness gave him no answers.

The next morning Phillips made a decision over a breakfast of fried eggs (two, over easy), bacon (well done), hash browns (crisp, lightly peppered), English muffins (buttered) and coffee (a dollop of Irish cream). He would discuss his situation with a priest today. "After all, they are sworn to confidentiality and are supposed to be good listeners. Just look at all those confessions they sit through."

Phillips tried to go to Catholic Mass once a week at a church just around the corner from where he lived. Generally he avoided going on Sunday lest he get caught up in the family crowd. Wednesdays always were good. The noon-time worshipers were generally pretty sparse, with some homeless thrown in who wanted to get out of the cold or rain or heat. Plus, there was always an all-you-can-eat spaghetti lunch afterwards for 3 bucks a head.

As the Mass began, he liked the priest who was preaching, Father Jonathan Luke. He had heard his sermons any number of times and thought them always relevant and thoughtful. Today's was exceptional. "Responsibility for your actions rests with you," Father Luke intoned. It was a warm day, and the crowd was thin. "The Lord teaches us that we alone will be the ones to answer at the hour of our death for what we did on this Earth. Some would blame their circumstances, their surroundings, their parents. Don't be foolish and believe this. Listen to your heart and your soul. Listen to the word of God. It is there and only there you will find answers.

"In the name of the Father and of the Son and of the Holy Spirit. Amen."

Phillips thought on this message as the Mass ended. He waited until Father Luke had shaken the hand of the last person to leave, then approached him.

"Father, I have something I would like to discuss with you."

The priest shook his hand firmly. "Yes?"

"But not here and not now. I am going out of town over the weekend and was wondering if we might have lunch next Tuesday."

"I can do that, yes."

"Wonderful. Is there any place you prefer?"

"Well, I am partial to Italian food, so perhaps Giuseppi's just up the street."

"I know the place. 1 p.m.?"

"You've got a date. See you there."

Phillips was glad already he had approached him. Brief and to the point.

He didn't have to be at Helena and Thomas's house for dinner until 7, which was a good thing since he was on dish duty for three hours that afternoon. Phillips had worked at Mark's, a down-home cafeteria-style restaurant on 14th Street, for half a dozen years, and he always enjoyed it there. Besides the perk of a free meal for each time he worked, he enjoyed the utter lack of pretentiousness you would expect to find in a lower-middle-class restaurant.

Phillips walked in. Felipe was on duty serving the main courses, Cassie filling the dessert shelves and salad bowls, Mark at the cash register. "Hey, kiddo, good to see you again," Mark, the owner, called to Phillips as he walked by. "Have something before you start." Since his shift was from 2 to 5 and it was only 1:30 now (another thing Phillips liked about Father Luke was that his Masses were short; today's was his customary 40 minutes) Phillips had time for lunch. Macaroni salad, a bowl of tomato and rice soup, Salisbury steak, a dish of chocolate pudding and a glass of Sprite. Mark's kept its menu short and its clientele moving by not requiring a whole lot of thought on what to take. At any one time there would 50 diners or so, which not only was good for Mark's business but also good for Phillips since there was a steady flow of dishes, and he liked keeping busy. Phillips had found the job when he was working to make ends meet as a struggling freelance travel writer. Now that he was into some pretty good money from his book and his improved income from travel writing, he could have easily walked away from the dishwashing job but didn't. He genuinely liked it here, and so he stayed.

His lunch finished while reading the *USA Today* Sports section, Phillips went into the back, put on his apron and began humping dishes. He liked the organization of the work, dumping leftover milk, water or whatever from the glasses, stacking dishes and separating utensils, then arranging everything in big trays that were pushed into the dishwasher. It was work that required constant movement but no real thought and gave Phillips time to fantasize, reflect or think of nothing at all, depending on his mood. Today he could have thought of many things – his failed relationship with Helena, his changing situation with Bea or his still-budding plan to do himself in next month because of this ugly intrusion of Alzheimer's into his neatly ordered world.

He decided to think of none of the above. Instead, he just talked aimlessly with the other dishwasher on duty, a college student named Simon. Phillips never really cared for him for no reason he could put his finger on. Simon had never done anything other than be a college kid, maybe a bit irresponsible at times and being preoccupied with food, sleep and sex, but who wasn't. None of those hurt Phillips other than him having to work a little harder to pick up the slack if Simon came to work a bit groggy under the spell of liquor or pussy from the night before. And there was certainly nothing wrong with that.

"Hi, Tom," he sang out as Phillips walked up and started his shift. "Simon," Phillips answered curtly.

"Tom, what do you think of suicide?"

"What, back here with the dishes?" Phillips tried to be flippant but was visibly startled by the question. How on earth could Simon possibly have known what was in the back of his mind?

"You're pretty funny, Tom. No, I meant as a concept. My summer Psychology class is discussing the subject and then we have to write a term paper on it. I just thought you were a pretty thoughtful guy and might have some ideas."

About the only serious discussion he and Simon had had up to this point was whether blonde or red pubic hair tasted better, so Phillips was a bit wary of where the guy was coming from. Still, the question seemed innocent even though two people raising the subject within 24 hours had to be more than coincidence. Was it an omen? Or was he just imagining things and making something from nothing?

"Simon, as a matter of fact I do have some strong feelings on the subject. And strangely, I was just talking about this last night with a friend of mine. I think people should be allowed to make their own decision on when it is time for their life to end. If they are sick or alone or just don't want to go on, that is their decision and theirs alone, and no state or government or law should have the right to tell them otherwise."

"You don't think killing yourself is murder nonetheless?" Simon asked as he pulled a steaming tray out of the washer and began piling the dishes on the metal shelves for drying.

"No, I think murder is when you take the life of someone else without their wishes. When you take your life out of your own free will and to accommodate your own desires, you are doing nothing more than if you move or take a new job. You are electing to do something."

"Cool, man. I never thought you were such a free thinker," Simon said. The two worked pretty much in silence the rest of the shift. There was a ton of dishes and not much time for coffeeshop talk about such weighty issues as when is the right time to die. But Phillips thought about the discussion as he methodically loaded the dishwasher with him and then as they emptied it and kept stacking the dishes for that night's dinner crowd. Finally it was 5 p.m., time to leave and go home to get ready for dinner that night for dinner with Helena and her family.

Phillips and Simon shook hands as they left, something they had never done. The discussion had left Phillips feeling a bit wistful, that perhaps Simon was all right after all. He even wished he had taken the time to get to know him a little better, realizing that if he carried through with his plan this would be the last discussion the two of them would ever have.

Phillips arrived at Helena's house at 7. He thought about her on the way over, how she used to call him "beloved," her gentle touch and understanding nature. He hadn't thought of those things all that much for a while, but now that maybe he really could have used someone strong in his life he thought of all the could-have-beens and never-would-bes with her.

Helena opened the door, smiling as always. "Hiya, Tom. The kids are waiting up to say good night to you before they go to bed."

Tom went into the living room, where Scarlett and Austin were in their pajamas watching Nickelodeon. "Yay, Uncle Tommy is here," they chimed in unison. "Hi, kids. How are my two favorites?" Phillips said and hugged them both. They each kissed him on the cheek, then ran up to Helena. "Off to bed the two of you. Your father is waiting for you in your bedroom." The kids pushed and pulled each other out of the living room, through the kitchen and up the stairs. "Good night, Uncle Tommy," they yelled.

"Whew, what a load. But I wouldn't have it any other way." Helena looked tired but had the radiance of a mother who loved her family and for whom tired was not allowed when it came to caring for those who made her life complete.

"Dinner will be ready in a bit. Have a seat and chat with me a little while. All well with you?"

"Sure, Helena. I'm going to Vegas for an assignment this weekend, then the middle of next week off on the driving trip back to Indiana to see my folks."

"That's right, and that reminds me." Helena walked over and picked up an envelope from the coffee table. "This is for you, but be sure not to open it until you're at your parents' house next month. And give them my love."

"OK and OK, love. What's for dinner?"

"Nothing fancy. Meatballs, mashed potatoes and gravy, peas, potato and leek soup, apple pie for dessert. In fact, make yourself comfortable and watch TV or something while I get everything ready. Thomas will be upstairs with the kids for a little while."

"Take your time."

Helena kissed him on the cheek and went into the kitchen. Phillips remembered Helena's excellent cooking. Nothing fancy, but always tasty, ample and filling. He could hear her whistling as she whipped up the mashed potatoes.

Phillips sat on the sofa and looked around the living room. He hadn't been over to their house in a while and the touches of a happy home, loving couple and family struck him as if he had seen them for the first time. Pictures of the four of them, a framed photo of Helena and Thomas on their wedding day, a picture of her pregnant with each of the kids. He picked up a vase. "Made in Mexico" was on the bottom. Phillips remembered the postcard he had gotten from them on their honeymoon to Acapulco. He ran his finger over the hutch with cups from New York, Chicago, San Francisco, a few other cities, nickel-and-dime mementos of trips for Helena and Thomas no one could put a price tag on.

Phillips felt a touch of melancholy. Maybe his solitary life with responsibilities to no one other than himself wasn't so fulfilling after all.

"Hey, Bea, your house looks real nice," Phillips called out. Helena stuck her head out of the doorway into the kitchen. "Tom, are you all right?"

"Sure, why do you ask?"

"You just called me Bea." Helena didn't have anything against Bea, and liked her in fact. But it was the first time he had mistakenly called her that.

"I did?"

"You surely did."

"Must have been just a slip. Sorry."

Helena returned to the kitchen. "Holy balls, how could I have done that?" Phillips said. He didn't know if the mistake was because of his diseased memory, he was actually thinking of Bea then or he had just made an honest mistake.

Still, it bothered him.

"Hi, Tom."

Phillips had been looking up at the ceiling in thought and didn't see Thomas come into the room. "Oh, hi, Thomas. Kids all tucked in?"

"That they are. I wouldn't trade them or their mother for anything."

"I don't see how you possibly could."

Thomas was always cordial to Phillips despite his past relationship with Helena. He was strong enough within himself and in his relationship with his wife that it didn't bother him, or at least never let on to Phillips that it did.

"Work going well?" Thomas asked.

"I have all the work I need, and what I do have I enjoy. And you?"

"Pretty much the same. I guess that makes us both very lucky."

Helena came into the room. "Dinner's all ready, guys. I thought we would be informal and eat in the kitchen tonight instead of the dining room."

Thomas kissed Helena and they held hands as the three of them went into the kitchen. It was redolent of Helena's exquisite meal, and Phillips was eager for the conversations the three of them so enjoyed with one another on politics, religion, sex, whatever. None of them was puritanical or rigid in their beliefs, so their good-natured debates and ribbing were pleasant and stimulating.

"Your kids seem to be doing well," Phillips said between mouthfuls.

"Tom, they are great kids. We are very fortunate," Helen said.

"Well, I just hope we are fortunate enough that they grow up to stay good kids," Thomas added. "Hey, honey, these meatballs are great," he said. Thomas lifted her hand regally and kissed it, leaving a thin film of gravy. "Oh, Thomas, cut it out," she said playfully and wiped herself with a napkin. "Children are a serious subject."

"So are meatballs," said her husband.

Thus fortified, they embarked on a round-the-table discussion.

Thomas: "I think parents can try their hardest and do their best and sometimes the kids still turn out bad because they fall in with the wrong crowd at school or just decide they aren't going to be good students."

Helena: "Parents have something to do with that. They can make them do homework or punish them if they don't, and watch out who they hang out with."

Thomas: "We can't police them 24 hours a day. Tom, what do you say about this?"

Phillips had been enjoying the meal and for once wasn't chiming in. He had been a good father to his Natalie, but he had to admit he hadn't been an everyday parent like Helena and Thomas and perhaps couldn't speak to the issue like they could. And in the past when he had, other parents had shot him down with their looks as being unqualified to judge since he wasn't in their shoes.

"Well," Phillips began. "you two are raising Austin and Scarlett and certainly know more what it's like to be a parent than I do. My only feeling is this: There is no guarantee that well-raised kids will turn out to be good and poorly raised kids will turn out to be bad. But being hands-on certainly does improve the odds.

"My strongest feeling is that parents too often throw up their hands and say kids will be kids, no matter what, and that kids have changed, they grow up faster, are exposed to all sorts of things we never were at their age.

"There may be more violence now on TV and in our schools. And they may be exposed to all sorts of unsavory influences on the Internet. But I firmly believe that children at heart remain immature beings that desperately want to be grown up but don't have the first idea what that means. It's not children who have changed, it's parents."

"What do you mean?" Helena asked.

"If I had tried one-tenth of the things I see and hear kids doing today my parents would have taken care of matters themselves. I think modern parents are afraid of disciplining their kids or won't take the time to do so, and if they did, they would find these kids react just as they did. Parents have given up and blame everyone else for the world's unruly monsters without looking in the mirror and realizing they themselves are at fault."

Helena and Thomas looked at each other and then at their friend. Phillips usually was pretty much shoot-from-the hip with them, intolerant with anyone who didn't think like him and disdainful of what he thought were abusive authority figures. His favorite target was politicians ("a bunch of chickenshit assholes who step up to the public trough once they get into office and forget who put them there"), but usually he had been pretty soft-spoken on the subject of kids.

"Tom, I'm not sure I totally agree with you, but much of what you say makes sense," Thomas finally said. "I do think parents sometimes pussyfoot around too much, try to reason when there is no reasoning to be done."

Helena looked at her husband and touched his hand. "Thomas, you're right. I just so hope our own two grow up to be good."

The three looked at each other and laughed. Even for them, this had been a weightier conversation than normal. Phillips had surprised himself, partly with the topic, but more with his commentary. "Maybe subconsciously this is how I want them to remember me, as a guy who could relate," Phillips said aloud as he drove home, smacking his lips over the dessert of apple pie with whipped cream that had been accompanied by coffee and a touch of brandy. Hugs at the door had concluded four wonderful hours together.

"For heavens sake, I'm already talking about myself in the past tense," he said as he drove up Pennsylvania Avenue. "Have I already convinced myself in my own mind that I'm going through with this?"

Phillips walked down the steps to his apartment frightened that he had made his decision and there was no turning back.

Wednesday, June 28

I had dinner with Helena and Thomas tonight and ended up coming home scaring the crap out of myself for thinking I was really going to through with this crazy ass idea of killing myself. Am I just being paranoid about this? Am I overreacting? Maybe Bea really could help me. And yet is that the way out, to rely on someone because I need their help rather than wanting to be with them? Do I want to be with Bea? Am I looking for a partner or a nurse? I don't know. I know I wish I had had the balls to stay with Helena, but after seeing her with Thomas and the two kids I know I could never have made her that happy or even kept my commitment to her. The story of my life, just playing with it and never taking it seriously. Here I am playing the role of some chickenshit Wild West gunman gonna blow my brains out. I've played with women, with sex, with career. I hit it lucky with my book and now just have taken it easy, never trying anything challenging or that required any commitment at all. Am I crazy to be thinking of doing this in my own parents' house?

Phillips put down his notebook, got out of bed and went to the closet again. He took out the gun and held it up. It gleamed in the reading light from his nightstand. As he turned the gun over in his hands, he liked its feeling of strength and finality, determined to take it along on his trip back to Indiana. He wrote again.

No! I'm going to do this. Why should I live to be an incoherent invalid? Why should I give my money to some nursing home to clean up my drool? I want to go out with head high and leave something to Natalie. She's got everything in my will. Give it to the living. And Mom and Dad would want to be there if I died of cancer, so why wouldn't they want to be there for this? Isn't this better than dying anonymous in some motel in an unknown town in the middle of nowhere? This all makes sense.

Phillips put away the gun and notebook, read a chapter from the novel and a passage from the Bible and turned off the light. He would be off to Las Vegas for his freelance assignment and had to pack and get to the airport by noon.

He slept soundly.

CHAPTER 10

LAS VEGAS

Phillips got up early Thursday, eager for his trip. He had been to Las Vegas half a dozen times over the years and always was ready for more. He liked it for the glitz, the anonymity, the cheap and abundant food, the gambling, and for him, a single man, the women with no strings attached. That is how Phillips had lived his life, or at least tried to, and it was, he supposed, why he was so happy. "Life with no strings. Can there be anything better?" Phillips mused over coffee, three eggs, half a dozen breakfast sausages and rye toast as he sat reading the sports pages to begin his day.

He looked up from the paper and thought of his changing life. "Life without strings is great until you find one day you need them and none are there. Or maybe you don't want them at all and find you are forced to have them. Then what? Well I know what." He put down his coffee, his eyes moistening. "I just won't live with this shit. I don't need it. I'll be damned if I'll turn into some invalid who needs help from a wife or some good-for-nothing nursing home worker to change my diaper.

"Shit on it. I'm going to Vegas, make some money, fill my belly and get laid."

With that, he finished off his breakfast and went to his bedroom to pack. Phillips was a light, but complete, traveler. He carried everything he would need in the way of toiletries right down to a book of matches in case he had to take a crap at the hotel. He packed nothing more than could be fit into a carry-on duffel bag, which for this trip meant three changes of slacks and Polo shirts, four days of underwear and a pair of shorts for walking the Strip in his spare time. He always brought his Bible along and on this trip had two extra passengers: his diary and the notebook he intended to carry with him with phone numbers and other details he used to keep in his head.

Phillips enjoyed his business trips to Vegas, and so must have the magazines that hired him for his freelance work there since they kept coming back to him. He smiled to himself at the thought of making a grand this weekend for just one article and shmoozing with a bunch of nerds over tech products he modestly understood and had no desire to own himself. Handheld organizers, cell phones, DVD players, set-top boxes were just so much junk for a generation that had too much money and not enough imagination to amuse itself without some tech toy along for the ride. Despite all the doomsaying talk that the tech boom couldn't go on forever, here in the middle of the year 2000, the New Millennium as some would call it, the spending merry-go-round was as strong as ever, the nerds everywhere, the dot-comers acting like they owned the world. "Frankly I don't give a shit about them or their products as long as the techie magazines keep coming along and paying me a thousand here and 800 there for writing some phony crud that makes some tech weenie hard," Phillips had said again and again to his drinking buddies, each time making himself laugh over the silliness of it all and more often than not closing with "it didn't matter." And it truly didn't.

Packed and ready to go, he hailed a cab and made his flight with plenty of time to spare. With the two-hour time difference, it was still only late afternoon when he was out of McCarran International Airport hailing another cab into downtown Vegas on a day and weekend full of promise. The temperature was a steamy 110 degrees as he climbed into the air-conditioned taxi.

"Circus Circus, please."

The cabby looked around. "For a moment I thought you were one of them nerds come to town for the convention, but you can't possibly be if you're staying at Circus Circus."

"Actually I am covering the convention for a magazine. Why are you so surprised that I would stay at Circus Circus?"

"Most of them stay at the fancier places since they're on expense accounts and want something impressive to bring hookers back to."

"I think you may be generalizing a bit there, friend."

"I don't know about this generalizing business, but I can say that for a lot of them this is the one time of the year they get laid."

True or not, Phillips and the cabby had a good laugh.

"Actually I stay at Circus Circus because I like seeing the circus acts and it's out of the way, and right next door they sell a huge chili dog that fills your belly for almost nothing."

"Buddy, you know how to live."

Phillips paid his fare and went into the hotel. He loved the scene. The lobby and casino beyond were full of people, young and old, most escaping something, a dreary job, a dull marriage, a life and world filled with monotony. Vegas held the promise of riches if you could hit a jackpot, and more important, it held the promise of excitement, which required no luck or jackpot but was there for the taking for anyone who came to the city of lights.

He checked in, went to a sumptuous buffet, took in some sights along the Strip, played the slot machines for a few hours and went to bed. Friday would be a workday, so there was no notebook tonight and only a little reading.

The convention center was packed as he arrived the next morning for a day of note-taking, product-checking and people-watching. He liked his magazine stories to be a blend of the convention's official purpose and the people who attended and made things happen. To do that he had to hang out in the aisles and booths, which he enjoyed doing so long as he didn't have to be with any one person for too long. There were suits, nerds, booths of all shapes and sizes, groupies, hangers-on and tech gadgets as far as the eye could see. Everything anyone could want, some of them even useful. Phillips had great respect for the business person who traveled or was otherwise heavily involved with his work and used technology to make his work easier or more effective. Likewise for technology nebishes like himself, the Internet for its instant communications, the PC for its versatility as a writing and e-mail tool and the cell phone for both the immobile and those on the go were all truly an advance in lifestyle.

But the person he had little use for was the one who hung a cell phone on his belt just to impress or bought a new tech toy just for the sake of owning it. He instantly recognized many of the same dot-comers who hung out back at the bar in D.C. They were the young twits who thought they knew everything, that HTML could substitute for a 3-inch dick or a big-screen TV would let them get away with having no manners or social skills.

Phillips waded into the crowd, pressed the flesh, took notes and mentally prepared the article he would write for the German magazine. He was pleased with himself.

The same couldn't be said for Bea. She had called in sick the Wednesday and Thursday after Phillips had told her of his Alzheimer's, and Friday wasn't much better. She reported to work but had a hard time concentrating. The hot, muggy Washington weather didn't help her mood. Aside from panties, damp clothing had never been her thing.

"Something wrong with your love life?" her boss had asked when she saw Bea, who came to work that morning looking pale and worn. "No, maybe something I ate," Bea lied. Normally Fridays were great for her.

After work and a nice dinner, she would head for one of the city's lesbian bars where she never failed to score and ended up spending the night in a no fuss-no muss sexual romp. But this Friday she was in a quandary over what to do about Phillips.

"Should I talk to him again when he gets back from Vegas? Should I tell him about my feelings? Would he even believe me or think I was just feeling sorry for him?" she asked herself taking a walk during her lunch break.

Finally she called Helena. They had become friends through Phillips and enjoyed each other's company, having lunch together on occasion. They also shared a mutual affection for their friend. After the usual pleasantries over the phone, Bea tried to get to the point without telling Helena anything about Phillips' Alzheimer's.

"Did you notice anything different about Tom this week when you had dinner and were drinking with him?" she asked.

"As a matter of fact I did, Bea."

Bea perked up. "Tell me about it."

"He got into a discussion with our friend Rodger about Jack Kevorkian. Then at dinner at our house he launched into this really serious discussion about parenting, and once he called to me from the living room and called me Bea."

"He did?"

"Yes. I thought maybe he was just tired. Is there more?"

"Helena, can we meet for lunch next week?"

"Sure. How about noon at Geno's, just around the corner from where I work?"

"I'll see you there."

Bea went home, signed on to her PC and searched for medical sites that gave details of Alzheimer's. Like many, she had heard of the disease and knew vaguely of its impact. But after going over several sites and reading of the stages and ultimate outcome, she sat back, cried softly and whispered: "I must help him."

Friday in Indiana was a pleasant one for Phillips' parents. Their routine was pretty much the same as it was every day. Peggy would rise early, tend to what needed to be done at home, then take the bus to the nursing home and share lunch with Joe. In mid-afternoon she would get back on the bus for the return trip home, rest in front of the TV and read the evening paper. Often in the summer she would sit in the swing in the back yard and watch the sun set, just as she and Joe had done all the summers of their marriage in this house. She and Joe had always loved the summer with its warm days, cool nights and gentle breezes.

Tonight as she sat in the swing she thought back on her life, thankful for all the good there had been. A bird sat singing on the clothesline. Peggy watched the sun as it sank beyond the horizon and hummed the catchy tune she used to sing to her Tommy when he was a little boy. And soon he would be home for a visit.

Before heading into the house for the night, she reached into her housecoat pocket and took out a cell phone, a gift from Tom and Kate a few Christmases ago. She called Joe.

"Good night, Joe, my love. See you tomorrow. I love you."

"Good night, my sweetheart. I love you," he answered.

Peggy ached at being away from Joe at night. This was not a routine she would have chosen, but she accepted it as a part of life and growing old. Joe felt the same. To her and to him, there was a constancy to life that gave it meaning, just as it always had. The circumstances may have changed, but their love for each other and their children was their guiding light. Each night before she went to sleep she read a Bible verse from Galatians that had hung over their bed since the day they returned from their honeymoon:

You have been given freedom, not freedom to do wrong, but freedom to love and serve each other.

"I wish Tom would marry," Joe said at lunch that day with his beloved wife. "It's not too late for him to find the right woman and carry on our family line." Joe only wanted for Tom what he had found himself: Happiness for a lifetime with a woman he loved, honored and cherished.

"Joe, that is for Tom to decide," Peggy answered. "Both of us liked Helena and for some reason that didn't work out. And at least he has his Natalie."

Both of them dearly loved Natalie and were very fond of both Helena and Bea. They were disappointed when both had said they probably couldn't come to the party next month.

"Whoever comes, it will be fine," Joe said to comfort Peggy.

In Vegas, it was getting late and Phillips had had enough of the rich and famously greedy. After a full day at the convention hall he had pressed enough flesh, seen enough technology gotta-haves and taken enough notes that he had a good start for his article. And besides, Saturday would be a special day.

CHAPTER 11

SHIRLEY TUCKER

Las Vegas energized Phillips. On Saturday, he was up at 6 a.m., before the hotel's wake-up call. He had a lot to do and wanted to get some time in outside before the day turned into its typical scorcher. He showered, then went to a Kinko's to see if he had any e-mail. There was just one message. It was from Bea.

"Tom, please call me as soon as you get back. Love, Bea"

"Shit, now what?" Phillips said as he left the building en route to a breakfast of a half-pound chili dog and a cup of coffee at a casino next to Circus Circus. "Not only is she messaging me, but she's calling me Tom. Whatever happened to Dick?"

He knew the answer. Telling Bea about his Alzheimer's had changed their relationship, perhaps forever. No longer were they two adults playing like kids with no cares, responsibilities or needs. This was now a life-and-death issue and not something that could be laughed off like most of the things in their friendly frolic.

Emotions were getting in the way, for both of them, and that was the last thing Phillips wanted. *I just want to get out of this as quickly and seamlessly as possible,* Phillips wrote in his diary last night after returning from the convention. This turn of events with Bea convinced him even more that ending his life now would be the right thing do to. "And yet," he admitted to himself as he took his first bite of the chili dog, "there's still a shred of doubt. Should I turn to Bea? Maybe I should have stayed with Helena…"

Now his mind was getting the best of him, something Phillips prided himself in beating. And he was determined to beat it again today.

The rest of the morning was spent playing small-change slot machines in Circus Circus, then taking a city tour of Las Vegas. He had always wanted to see Liberace's house, one of the stops, and was as star-struck as the others on the bus were when they drove past the homes or one-time homes of other celebrities in the city like Johnny Carson.

Lunch was at his favorite place in town, the Luxor Hotel's buffet. A couple of plates full of fried potatoes, Italian sausage, chicken, pasta, macaroni salad and minestrone soup put him back in the frame of mind he had when he began the day: another afternoon at the convention to complete his interviews and sorting through the new products, followed by a night at a strip-tease palace and the coup de grace, a lap dance by a red-headed vixen named Desiree.

The convention center was packed when he arrived Saturday afternoon. He'd already talked to enough of the vendors and visitors but wanted one last interview. He spotted him quickly, a young fellow who looked to be in his mid-20s. "Perfect," Phillips said as he walked over and introduced himself.

"Hi, my name is Tom Phillips and I'm doing a piece on this convention for a German electronics magazine and was wondering if I could have a few minutes of your time."

The man turned and smiled, looking Phillips in the eye. He was wearing a white cotton shirt, beige Dockers and dark brown moccasins. Up close, he looked even younger than he'd seemed to Phillips from across the room.

"Hi, I'm Michael Smithson. What can I do for you?"

"Well, Mike ..."

"It's Michael."

"Michael, I was wondering what you were hoping to get out of this show."

"Are you going to quote and name me?"

"I was hoping to."

"Sure, why not? I am here because I am looking for a cell phone that connects to the Internet and to e-mail."

"Why would something like that be necessary to you?" Phillips' critical tone caught Smithson off guard.

"You seem to think I am evil or something because I am looking for this product."

"Not evil. I just wonder why you would feel such a constant need to be connected this way. I always check my investments in the newspaper. What's wrong with still doing it that way?"

The crowd milled about them. A coffee wagon came by and Phillips bought one for him and for Smithson.

"Well, Thomas ..."

"It's Tom."

"Well, Tom, I am sure your grandfather or great-grandfather traveled by horse. So by your logic, were your father and you wrong by using a car? Things change. Society progresses."

"Would you say our society has progressed?"

Smithson smiled slightly. "I thought this was going to be a product interview, and here we are debating the progress or lack thereof of Western civilization."

"It's not a debate. I have my own observations, and I want to know how they square with other people's ideas."

"And what are your observations?"

"That we live in era of delusion. We call used cars pre-owned, 800-square-foot bandboxes apartment homes. Stocks will never fall, more is always better. People never die."

"Man, Tom, you sure are bitter for someone still so young."

"Do I seem bitter?"

"What else would you call it?"

"Realistic."

Smithson laughed. Phillips, after his initial coolness, was beginning to like this man, or at least warm to him for being candid and willing to fight back to his arguments. "I never write these articles to be just another product rundown. I like to give them some context and make the readers think about the products they want to use and whether they really want or need them."

"Here's another thing to consider then," Smithson answered back. "Decades ago, people lived in Vegas in its sweltering heat without air-conditioning. Should they have turned their back on it when it came along because air-conditioning was something new to them, that it represented change?"

"Tell me," Phillips countered, "just why is that fancy cell phone so important to you? Why the need for the latest bell and whistle?"

Smithson looked serious and a little sad. "Actually it's because my mother has Parkinson's. She wants to e-mail me whenever she feels lonely or in pain, and by being mobile I could answer her right away. As for the Internet, I just like to keep track of my investments. I make good money for a tech firm and am hoping to move her closer to where I live so I can care for her better. My dad died last year and she really has no one.

"I realize it's obsessive to keep checking on my investments this way since I doubt I would ever just sell anything based on a price I see during the day like this. Maybe it just makes me feel a little better about my mom to think I have control over things that will help her."

Phillips extended his hand. "Michael, thanks for your candid comments. They will help me a lot in my writing of this convention."

"That's it?" Smithson asked. He seemed almost disappointed the interview was over. "Good luck to you, Tom, and try not to be so hostile and critical."

"We'll see."

As Phillips left the convention center he turned and looked for Smithson, who was watching him. They waved to each other, and Phillips left and headed back to his hotel.

It was late afternoon when he returned to his room, still time for a nap, some TV and dinner. But first he wanted to start his magazine article while the ideas were fresh in his head. Phillips sat at his laptop and started to write.

By Tom Phillips

We the wireless, plugged-in, on-the-go society of the New Millennium can't raise children anymore or start marriages that last or solve world poverty or for that matter even cure the common cold.

Why is that?

Is it perhaps that in our constant effort to stay in motion we have forgotten the beauty of standing still, of appreciating life for its own sake, of realizing that life does end and that we need to make the most of it while we are here?

I have just spent part of two days here at the latest tech convention in Las Vegas talking to vendors and customers and looking over the products that are supposed to make our lives better. I come away convinced that only if we let them make our lives better will these products truly be considered progress.

Consider Michael Smithson, a young professional here to buy an Internet- and e-mail enabled telephone that will help him take care of his ailing mother. In the hands of a man such as this, technology breakthroughs truly are just that.

It is up to each of us to make them so.

Phillips read over his introduction and liked it. He continued by listing what he considered to be the five most useful products to come out of the convention and the five least useful from the perspective of their potential impact or potential uselessness for society, threw in some more quotes from vendors and customers, put in a little color about the dot-comers (though he didn't call them that), spell-checked the puppy and shot it to Germany.

That night, his German editors sent an e-mail very pleased with the article and asking when he would write again. But Phillips wasn't there. He was at a gentleman's club up Las Vegas Boulevard where the tourist families didn't venture and the dot-comers didn't know about yet.

The Bottoms Up Club was rocking.

He paid his $10 cover charge and walked upstairs into a dimly lit room upholstered and carpeted in red. In the center of the room was a fireman's pole and around it was wrapped a naked blonde, dancing outrageously to the sound of La Belle's *Voulez vous*. Perhaps in high school or even in college the woman had been a gymnast because she lifted her right leg straight up that flagpole to split her crotch for all to see. Around a circular stage sat perhaps a dozen men watching her every move. They watched with lurid interest as she walked over and then knelt in turn in front of each one and opened her legs so they could see halfway up the inside of her stomach, to say nothing of every line, crevice, hair and dimple in her pussy. Dollars, fives and 10s were thrown onto the stage. No one touched her. Two men got up with lumps in the front of their pants and headed to the rest room.

Phillips sat in the back at one of the tables, and even from that vantage point got aroused. A woman wearing only bikini panties came over. "Hi, my name is Cherie. What can I get you to drink? Two are with the cover," she said brightly and winked. "I'll be over later if there is anything else you need."

Phillips ordered two 7 and 7's and looked around, hoping he would see Desiree.

Desiree Gordon, at least that is how she had introduced herself, was an entertainer and waitress at the club. When she wasn't showing her charms to the men sitting around the stage she was taking drink orders, and if she appealed to one of the patrons and he to her, she would take him to a back room for a lap dance. It cost 80 bucks plus a tip if you wanted her to strip and squirm on your crotch until you got off in your pants. It wasn't the real thing, but it was safe and had an eroticism all its own. That's what Phillips had imagined, since he had never done it though he had wanted to. And tonight he aimed to overcome his fears and make it happen. "What have I got to lose? I'll never be here again anyway," he said half out loud as he sipped on the first of his drinks.

Then he saw her. Desiree came in from a back room and was recognizable to anyone who knew her. Flaming red hair, long shapely legs and deep cleavage, she left nothing to the imagination tonight because all she wore were a white G-string and a pair of navy blue fuck-me shoes. Whether the color combination between her hair, panties and shoes was intended or accidental, Phillips still proclaimed her a patriot. He wondered if Desiree moaned *The Star-Spangled Banner* while she was getting porked.

Phillips was surprised when she came over and was astonished when she offered her hand and said, "Tom, nice to see you again. It's been a while."

Phillips took her hand. "Actually it's been almost a year. I'm glad you're here tonight, and I'm amazed you remember my name."

"Some faces you don't forget," she said and took a measure of delight in giving him a steamy look. "You old prick-teaser you," she said to herself. "What was that?" Phillips asked innocently, draining his drink. "I was just saying to myself that I'm glad you're here too," she answered.

Phillips had met Desiree on his last business trip to Vegas. He liked the way she danced, the way she moved, the way she looked, the way she talked. He had almost taken her back for a lap dance but at the last minute backed out because of a fear of getting caught, a feeling he somehow was sinning, a feeling maybe that this was wrong though he didn't know why.

Desiree brought Phillips out of his reverie over his last trip by pushing her ample bosom and cherry red nipples within three inches of his face, focusing her deep green eyes on his and asking, "Is there anything I can do for you tonight?"

"As a matter of fact, after I finish this drink, there is."

She smiled, took him by the hand and said, "Bring it along."

The room was small, maybe 12 feet by 12 feet. Inside were a chair and sofa, both upholstered in red velvet. Phillips was uneasy but determined to stick with his plan for the lap dance tonight.

Desiree led him to the sofa.

"Any particular song you want me to play?" She smiled and flirted with him.

Phillips thought for a second. "How about *Last Dance* by Donna Sommer?"

"Sounds like a winner to me, white man. Let me go find it."

She went over to a closet door hidden behind a curtain, looked over stacks of CDs and took out the one she wanted. She held it up for Phillips to see. "Here it is. Get ready to be done in your pants."

"What should I do?"

"Just relax, hon. I'll do the rest."

Phillips was so aroused he was afraid he would come then and there. He took a breath, sipped his drink and thought of his parents' house in Indiana. Why he'd think of that when he was about to get jacked off in his drawers by a woman he had talked to no more than five minutes total was a mystery to him. Whatever, it calmed him and he was ready to go.

The music started. Desiree came toward him as he sat on the couch, reached out to him, took his hand and led him to the chair. He walked along meekly. His knees shook. "Relax, handsome," Desiree chirped above the music. She walked over to the CD player, turned it lower, then looked him in the eye, dropped her panties and walked toward him. She put her left foot on his leg, unstrapped a shoe, then did the same thing with her right. Desiree began to dance, slow, erotic movements not two feet in front of him. She danced closer and closer, pushed his legs together, strad-dled him and lowered herself so her crotch was touching the erection in his pants. Phillips said nothing, just sat there like he was ready to explode. Desiree opened her mouth and put out her tongue. He touched it with his, looked deeply into her eyes and shot in his pants.

Desiree backed away. Phillips sat there not knowing what to do. He hadn't choked the bishop so he didn't have to wash his hands. He hadn't screwed her so he didn't have to ask if she enjoyed it. So he did nothing and just basked in the moment. "I finally had a red head," he whispered. Phillips felt good. He smiled.

"What do I owe you?" he asked after a moment.

"Eighty dollars, hon," Desiree said as she slipped her panties back on and went to pick up her shoes.

Phillips reached into his pocked, took out a wad of money and peeled off two $100 bills.

"Buy yourself something nice."

"That's real nice of you. I hope you come back to see me real soon."

Phillips looked at Desiree, looked around the room, looked down at the stain on his pants. He was proud of himself.

On a whim, he blurted, "What are you doing tomorrow?"

Desiree looked at him suspiciously, said nothing at first, then "I'll probably watch a baseball game or something since it's my day off. Why?"

"I was just wondering if you'd like to drive to Laughlin with me?"

"Where's Laughlin?"

"You live here and you don't know where Laughlin is?"

"Look, I work six days a week and just trying to regain my senses on the seventh. If you want to get accusatory about it, you can leave now."

"I'm sorry. I was just thinking of going to Laughlin tomorrow and wanted to know if you wanted to come along. Laughlin's about a 90-minute drive from here right through the desert. It's a great place on the Colorado River. We could go in the morning and come back in the late afternoon. I have to fly back to Washington soon anyway."

"You know, I've talked to you these past two times and spent this dance in with you here just now and I never knew where you were from."

"So do you want to go?"

"Why not?"

"Meet you here at 9 tomorrow morning?"

"Sure, hon."

Desiree saw Phillips to the door and waved to him as he left. He wasn't even sure Desiree would show up and half-hoped she wouldn't. But when Phillips arrived at 9 the next day, there she was in the parking lot, wearing sandals, jeans and a T-shirt with the words Party Till You Puke.

"Nice outfit," Phillips said as she got into the car.

"Don't you like it? I can change if you want."

"No, I said it was nice."

"Maybe you're lying."

"Maybe. I picked up sandwiches and sodas, Desiree. Have some."

Desiree dug eagerly into the bag, took out a sandwich and Coke and smiled. "Name's Shirley, Shirley Tucker."

Phillips laughed. "Your name is Shirley Tucker? Why the Desiree business?"

"How many guys would want someone named Shirley to sit on their laps and get them off? Shirley's the name of a girl everyone went to high school with."

Phillips had to admit she had a point.

The drive through the desert was wonderful. There was little traffic, and the sun ruled a cloudless sky. Nobody knew them, and they knew nobody. It was perfect.

Shirley talked about herself.

"I came here three years ago to make enough so my boyfriend and I could buy a house back in Omaha. That's where I'm from and where he is still. One more year and Bruce and I will be set."

"He's waited for you all this time?"

"Sure, we've waited for each other. Twelve more months and the wait will be over. We'll have the rest of our lives together, and the time here will have been worth it."

"He doesn't mind that you do this?"

"He doesn't know." Shirley looked out the window.

"Do you like it here?" Phillips asked.

She snorted. "What do you think? You're one of the very few who has ever asked me to go anywhere without wanting to get into my pants. That's why I agreed to go today. I trusted you."

"Thank you. You're right about me."

Phillips and Shirley spent their day in Laughlin gambling, eating and talking. She never asked about him, and he never volunteered. For all she knew, Phillips was just another dot-comer in town to get his pants messy and then go home. But one time she glanced at him and decided Phillips was all right. She was glad she had lap danced him.

He dropped her off in the parking lot of Bottoms Up. They waved to each other as she got into her car. Shirley drove into the street and then was gone.

Phillips returned to the hotel. His diary entry for the day was simple: *Shirley Tucker? Man, life is strange.*

Chapter 12

▼

FATHER LUKE

Phillips returned to Washington on Monday. The day turned out to be relaxing and uneventful and was capped by a homemade dinner of two cube steaks, lightly peppered, on Kaiser rolls with butter, spicy German mustard, onions and a thick layer of dill pickles. Joined by a helping of French fries, two ears of corn and two bottles of ginger ale, the dinner made Phillips feel like he was knocking on heaven's door. He fell asleep watching a ball game on TV, his peace of mind returned, if only for the day, as he drifted off.

Neither Phillips nor Father Luke had realized their lunch date was set for July 4 when they made it, but neither had anyplace else they had to go so it seemed as good a time as any to get together. Father Luke was waiting outside the restaurant when Phillips arrived at noon on Tuesday.

Phillips extended his hand. Father Luke shook it firmly. "Father, thank you for meeting me today. I thought maybe you would want to join some of the city's festivities," Phillips said to the priest as they walked into the restaurant.

"No problem at all. I will probably watch some fireworks tonight but now am just as happy meeting with you. You are Thomas, right? May I call you that?"

"Of course. May I call you Jonathan?"

"You may call me Father Luke."

Father Jonathan Luke was 34 years old and sturdy in faith, mind and body. The priest was 6 foot 3, 230 pounds, had steel-gray eyes, coal-black hair and bore a striking resemblance to John F. Kennedy Jr. Phillips could swear that he had once been a football player. "My God," he thought to himself as the two of them were shown to their table, "if this guy weren't a priest he could be getting pussy from here to Timbuktu."

Out of coincidence or perhaps sensing what was going through Phillips' mind, the priest smoothed out a crease in the tablecloth with his right hand and began. "Let's talk about ourselves, Thomas. Shall I start?"

"Absolutely."

"My name is Jonathan Luke. With a name like that you would think I was probably ordained from birth to become a priest, and maybe you would be right." He paused as the waitress came by with a glass of water for each. Even though his priest's collar was plain for all to see, her eyes lingered as she walked away.

"But my becoming one was not always so obvious. I got a football scholarship out of high school and became the starting middle linebacker at the University of Michigan in my junior year." Phillips smiled.

"My senior year I was a second-team All-American, and off the field I was an all-star womanizer. In my four years of playing, I had managed to bed a woman from every one of the Big Ten schools, and to make some money I was a stripper at private parties. I charged a hundred bucks a show and told whoever arranged the party that I got to pick one woman to go home with. I never went to bed alone those nights."

Phillips listened.

"Though I would have never imagined it happening, my life changed when we went to the Rose Bowl that year. The coach arranged for some of the players to visit a children's hospital in L.A. during the week leading up to the game and I went along since it beat watching TV.

"When I saw those children, those small gifts from God there lying in bed, many of them dying without ever having had a chance to live, I was numbed, humbled and angry. That night I knelt at my bed and sobbed for those children and for myself. And I knew that while God wasn't responsible for their sickness, he made us responsible for caring for those children, for comforting them and for loving them. That very night, on my knees, I decided to enter the priesthood and have never looked back."

"Did you still play in the Rose Bowl?" Phillips asked.

"Of course I did. Made seven unassisted tackles. I even cold-cocked the UCLA quarterback with probably the best hit of my life, knocked him clean out of the game for five minutes. Years later we ran into each other at a convention, he's a motivational speaker now, and he told me I hit him so hard he couldn't remember his name for a while."

The look in Father Luke's eyes told Phillips that the priest would be forever proud of that game.

"Shall we eat?" the priest asked after a pause as their waitress walked up.

"By all means."

Father Luke ordered soft-shelled crab, shrimp and ricotta cheese served on a bed of lettuce for the starter, followed by veal in a lemon butter and wine sauce with capers along with rice pilaf for the main course. Phillips ordered the homemade soup (minestrone) for himself and ribbon pasta with tomato sauce, mozzarella cheese and basil for he and Father Luke to share. For his main course he selected rolled smoked ham filled with Monterey Jack cheese and green onions sautéed in a fresh mushroom sauce, accompanied by parsley-buttered potatoes. A bottle of red wine completed their meal.

The two men, their order complete, sat back with a contented look on their faces, sipped water and broke off chunks of bread that they dipped in olive oil. Did the founding fathers have life so good?

Father Luke broke the silence.

"So tell me, Thomas, what is on your mind?"

"Father, I don't want to get into the specifics, but I'll just say that I have a medical condition and don't know how to cope with it."

"Do you have AIDS?"

Phillips was shocked by the question. "Of course not."

"I just thought I would ask. You wouldn't be the first person to come to me with that issue, Thomas."

"I hadn't really thought about that, but no, I definitely don't have AIDS. I have something that will develop long term and I don't know how to handle it. I have no family I would want to take care of me, to burden them with this, and the prospect of handling this myself is equally distasteful."

Father Luke bit off a piece of bread and washed it down with a drink of the wine that had arrived while Phillips was talking.

"Thomas, you talk of having a loved one care for you in time of need as a burden. Is it not possible they would welcome it as a means of showing or accepting their love for you?"

"I couldn't be sure of that, Father, and I don't want to depend on anybody."

"Well since you are so independent, don't you think you have the fortitude to see if through yourself?"

"I'm not sure."

"Thomas, my life stands for doing the work of the Lord. What does yours stand for?"

Phillips looked off and didn't answer.

"Maybe this is part of your problem."

Phillips shifted in his chair.

"Do you read the Bible?"

Phillips perked up. "I do, chronologically. I try to read some each night and have already read it through a couple of times."

"That seems sort of haphazard to me in finding a message to sustain you in times of trouble. I have favorite passages I can turn to in times of need, or indeed times of celebration. My favorite is 2 Timothy 4:7-8. Do you know it?"

"No, Father."

Father Luke's eyes glistened as he recited the passage:

I have fought the good fight, I have finished the race, I have kept the faith. Henceforth there is laid up for me the crown of righteousness, which the Lord, the righteous judge, will award to me on that Day, and not only to me but also to all who have loved his appearing.

"Think of the Bible as a source of exultation and comfort, Thomas. It's not a novel."

"You may have a point."

Phillips and Father Luke talked on during their meal but turned to lighter subjects of baseball, travel and life in D.C.

Over coffee they turned serious again.

"Thomas, what do you do for a living?"

"I am a freelance travel writer."

"Sounds interesting."

"It is. I get good assignments, just got back from Las Vegas, in fact."

"You can support yourself on freelance travel assignments?"

"Actually I made a real killing on the one novel I wrote, *The Awakening*. I did it under a pen name, Philip Sandman."

The priest looked at him. "You are Philip Sandman?"

Phillips was surprised. "Yes, I am. Why?"

"I read your book and liked it very much. But I thought your name was Thomas."

"I used a pen name so people wouldn't know I wrote it. It wasn't provocative?"

"Some scenes are, but overall I enjoyed the book's message of rebirth."

"I wouldn't think you could enjoy a book with sex scenes like the ones I wrote."

Father Luke chuckled. "Thomas, I am a priest and a man, not a corpse."

Phillips asked for the check.

"I'd like to chat a bit more with you over coffee if you like," Father Luke said.

"Absolutely."

"Thomas, if there is one thing I want to leave you with today it would be a spirit of hope. You feel burdened and that you would be a burden, but nobody is forever in a situation like that. You can relieve yourself of these feelings and like the main characters in your book, find a rebirth in your life.

"All you need to do is recognize the sign God is sending you."

"What do you mean, a sign?"

"I believe that at turning points in our lives, God sends us a sign that he means for us to take a new path. It is up to us to recognize that sign, and having seen it, realize it for what it is and accept it.

"For the main characters in your book, it was them finding each other. For me, it was going to that children's hospital and seeing those young ones in need those many years ago. The sign is never the same, and the acceptance of it can be very different.

"To some, like those in your book, the sign is an awakening, as you so aptly put it, and their lives change over time. To others, like myself, the sign is a spark that ignites a rebirth."

"Whichever it is, you and you alone must recognize it and act upon it."

"Is the sign obvious?"

"It should be, but many overlook it or refuse to accept it. The sign won't necessarily be something that bites you on the nose. Indeed, it might be the slightest of things. But if the heart and soul are receptive, the sign is there, waiting."

"Well, Father, I'm not so sure about this, but I will try."

"Do more than try, Thomas."

They finished their coffee, walked out of the restaurant and shook hands in the hot afternoon sun.

"Father, may I call you in the days ahead if I need to talk?"

"By all means, though I will be in Chicago the next two weeks visiting my sister."

"Hey, I'll be in Chicago too on the way to my parents' house in Indiana. May I try you at your sister's?"

Father Luke wrote the phone number on a business card, handed it to Phillips and shook his hand again. "God be with you, Thomas. Be strong. Be faithful. And look for your sign. It often comes when we least expect it."

Phillips watched the priest walk around the corner, then went to his car and drove home.

A couple of blocks away, another conversation was taking place at Geno's over Caesar salad, pizza and white wine.

"Helena, I am sure happy you were able to meet me here today. I have something important I need to talk about, and you are the only one I can confide in."

"Bea, I am glad I could make. It sounded serious on the phone. Besides, my husband always likes to have some time alone with the kids, so they're at a park near our house and I don't have to rush at all. Now, how can I help you?"

Bea looked out the window, then down at her salad. Tears ran down her cheeks.

Helena reached across the table and held Bea's hands in hers. "What on earth is the matter?"

"It's Tom."

"Tom?" Helena pulled her hands back and looked at Bea. "What about Tom?"

"You must promise not to tell anyone what I will tell you now."

"I promise."

"We went to dinner recently, and Tom told me he has Alzheimer's disease."

"What? It … it can't be." Helena put the palm of her hand to her mouth and started to sob. "I sensed something was wrong with him at dinner the other night, but nothing like this. My God."

Now Bea reached across the table and held Helena's hands. "He won't let anybody help him. He won't even tell his parents. I'm worried about him. I want to help him so. Helena, I truly love Tom. What can I do?"

Helena said nothing for a moment. She was recalling her own feelings for Tom, a time when they were happy and in love, even a momentary pang of jealousy with Bea's own declaration. Helena looked at Bea, took a sip of wine and spoke.

"Bea, you know of my own romantic involvement with Tom and how I still love him in my own way to this day. But ours was a love that could never be. Yours may be one that still could happen. I can't tell you what to do about this, but I think you have to go to him and try to make him know how you feel and that you will care for him and love him unconditionally."

She looked into Bea's eyes. "Bea, the times I have been happiest in my life is when I gave too much and the saddest when I gave too little."

Bea wiped her eyes. "Yes, I must, I must go to him….I know. I will go to his parents' house and meet him there next week and see how we can together deal with this. Thank you, Helena, thank you."

"No, Bea, thank you for loving our Tom."

After his lunch with Father Luke, Phillips went home, took a nap, then ordered a pepperoni pizza with thick crust from the Inferno, a neighborhood pizzeria. He took a Coke from the refrigerator and settled in front of his PC as he waited for the pizza to be delivered. He stared and waited. "Well…shit." Phillips couldn't remember his password.

"I guess I didn't start this notebook for nothing," he said and took out the pad from a desk drawer. There was the entry on the first page. "Password: Helena."

Phillips logged on. There was the usual spam on how get a cheaper mortgage, watching a teenage girl masturbate and how to get yourself a bigger pecker. And there was a message from Dr. Byron Frank. Phillips opened it.

Hi, Tom:

It's me, Dr. Frank. I hope you are well and thinking positive thoughts. Tom, I certainly understand how this development with your health is alarming to you. I have had many patients in similar circumstances. I just say again that there is plenty of medical help available, counseling and support groups are flourishing, and advances in treatment are being pursued around-the-clock. I have included several attachments with this note telling you of some promising research. Also, I encourage you to tell a small circle of people upon whom you rely emotionally, perhaps your parents, close friends, a significant other if you have one.

In the meantime don't hesitate to call on me at any time. I recall you said you were heading back to Indiana sometime soon, so I wish you a safe and happy journey. Be sure to stop in and see me as soon as you get back.

Happy July 4th!

Byron Frank

"Fuck a support group," Phillips said and smiled thinly with the expectation that he would never be coming back. He opened one of the attachments. It was about new guidelines on the recognition and treatment of Alzheimer's and included details on a class of drugs called cholinesterase inhibitors along with the notation that they had proven effective in improving memory and abilities of people with mild to moderate symptoms. It also suggested Vitamin E as a means of easing the disease's symptoms.

Phillips deleted the note and attachment and stared at the wall. "I'll be taking my .357-caliber vitamin any day now and won't need any more of these chickenshit remedies."

The pizza arrived. He ate it in front of the TV, cleaned up, then went out to see the city's July 4th festivities.

Phillips had always liked the fireworks. July 4th was one of his favorite holidays because it was such a happy day and brought people outside for family, barbecues and good times. As he sat on the front lawn of a church and watched the fireworks explode with the Washington Monument as a backdrop, Phillips clapped with the rest of the onlookers. He thought of his trip and how he looked forward to driving back to Indiana, yet felt a twinge of sadness with the realization he would not be coming back here, never to see this fireworks spectacle again, never to enjoy a warm Washington evening again, never to be a carefree soul again.

Phillips walked home, feeling sad and alone.

Bea didn't go out for fireworks, didn't call a friend, didn't watch TV. She sat on the balcony of her apartment overlooking the Tidal Basin as the sun set. She picked up the phone.

"Oh, hi, Ben, I didn't know if you'd be home."

"Hi, Bea. I had lunch with some friends and was just going to enjoy the evening at home."

"Ben…"

"Yes, Bea?" Ben knew what was coming, had expected it from the first time they had spent time together.

"Ben, I have to leave you. I am in love with someone and he needs my help and I must go to him."

"Bea, I have known from the start there was another in your heart, even though you may not have known it yourself."

"You did?"

"Of course, my love. It was quite evident."

"Ben, I'm sorry to hurt you."

"Bea, how could you hurt me? You gave my life love and energy and fun, and for that I will always be grateful for the time we had. I will always remember you."

"Goodbye, Ben."

"Goodbye, my dear."

Bea hung up the phone and stared at it for a moment. "I love you, Big Gray."

Ben went to his balcony and looked up at the moon, his eyes misting. "I love you, Honey Bea," he whispered to the stars.

Tom was sitting up in bed, reading finished. He looked off, thinking to himself how much life had changed in nine short, and yet eternally long, days. He began to write.

Tuesday, July 4

I am finally beginning to see how smug and complacent I have been these years. Or was I happy and content? Is there anything wrong with that? Where does happy end and smug begin? Is the way I feel any reason to die? What about a couple married 20, 30, 40 years and one of them dies? Should the other die too because that happiness has ended? Or should the person just find another happiness? But is that possible? For them, is it happiness ended, or happiness interrupted? I want to die, and yet I want to live. But I can't stand the idea of living this way. Is God tapping me on the shoulder and telling me to get serious? I'm looking forward to my trip, to see Mom and Dad again, Natalie and Kate. But I know how it will end, unless I see the sign Father Luke talked about. The sign. Could this be for real?

CHAPTER 13

▼

LEAVING

Phillips prepared to leave D.C., a trip from which he was certain he would never return. Wednesday would be a busy day. He had to map out his itinerary, call Natalie, Kate, Bea and Mom and Dad and leave things in his apartment just right so that Mr. Jones could take care of his effects and get the place ready for the next tenant without undue fuss.

Russell Jones, the landlord, was a pleasant enough person, a reason Phillips didn't want to leave him hanging. The rent was fair, there were no petty rules or interferences and the place was free of cockroaches. Phillips tapped out a note on his PC:

Dear Mr. Jones

When you read this I will be dead. Really. Don't be alarmed, shocked or sad. I chose to go out this way and I am at peace now. (I hope!) Anyway, I have left the apartment clean. Just take my things and give them to the

Salvation Army or take what you want and throw away the rest.

I have enjoyed living here.

Sincerely,
Tom Phillips

Phillips printed out the note, put it in an envelope addressed to the landlord and left it on the dining room table. He put it there confident Jones wouldn't come into his apartment and find it prematurely since in all the years Phillips had lived there, not once had his landlord come into the place uninvited. Certainly after he died, either Helena or Bea would get in touch with Jones, tell him what had happened and Jones would take things from there once he came into the apartment and found the note. That taken care of, Phillips went back to his desk and took out a notebook to begin writing down his travel itinerary back to Indiana. As much as he liked his PC, Phillips still liked the personal touch now and then, writing down things, doing things by hand.

"Speaking of which," he said as he opened his notebook, then put it back and went into the bathroom to continue his love affair with the toilet bowl. By his rough calculations, he was up to episode number 8,456,321. Phillips dropped his pants, sat on the toilet and let his imagination go to work as he stroked himself.

He had seen a young blonde yesterday while watching the fireworks, and she had set his blood to racing since. He imagined her now, she a high school prom queen, he a chaperone, she a teenager (18 years old, of course), he a 40something, the two of them having carried on a flirtatious fling for some time and this night planning to do something about it. After the dance he had driven her to his brother's apartment, where the Little Miss Perfect Prom Queen would turn into Miss Senior Class Slut who had wanted to bang an older man for some time and tonight intended to make it so. He went down on her on the floor the minute the door closed behind him and she mounted him there without even taking off her dress. As he shot in her, she cried out, "Oh, Daddy," and just at that point Phillips consummated his daydream.

Phillips looked at his watch. Thirty-eight seconds from start to finish. "Brother, you have staying power," he said and laughed. But then as he sat there in the afterglow of yet another date with his fist, Phillips reflected on what he would miss after he took his own life, other than the people who mattered to him. In no particular order, he made a mental list: Food, pussy, baseball, beating off, music, the Bible.

Phillips got up, flushed away the memory of Little Miss Perfect Prom Queen and went back to his desk.

Bea was busy too. She dialed, then listened to the telephone ring at Phillips' parents' house, hoping they would be there.

"Hello?"

"Oh, hello, Mrs. Phillips, I'm glad I found you at home. This is Bea Farmer."

"Bea, how lovely to hear from you." Phillips' parents had always been fond of Bea, although they had never thought of her as a potential partner for their son the way they had of Helena. Still, they liked her, particularly since she addressed them as Mr. and Mrs., a symbol of formality and respect in an age when both were in short supply.

"I do hope you are calling, Bea, to say you can come on the 15th."

"I was calling to say that very thing. And how is Mr. Phillips?"

"He is fine, and I am sure he will be even better when I tell him the good news about your coming."

"I'm looking forward to it. I will see you then, Mrs. Phillips. "

"Goodbye, honey. Looking forward to seeing you again."

"Till then. Bye."

After hanging up, Peggy called Joe. "Hello, my love. Bea just called to say she's coming. Won't that be nice?"

"Bea, Bea, tell me who she is again?"

Peggy wasn't bothered by her husband's forgetfulness from time to time. He was entitled, she would tell herself, and besides he had other health issues to be concerned with. She was just glad she could still call him and see him and love him and get through to him with a little careful explanation. And Peggy was very happy the get-together with Tom back in town was getting bigger.

"Bea is one of Tom's friends from Washington. She is that nice girl with the short haircut you always got a kick out of."

"Oh, yes, now I remember. I am glad she is coming too. It will be so nice to see our Tommy again, won't it, love? Will I see you later?"

"I'll be there. Till then, my husband, I love you."

"Goodbye, my sweetheart."

Joe looked out the window, smiling at having talked to his wife and thinking ahead to seeing his son.

Bea decided it was time for some action. After hanging up from her conversation with Phillips' mother, she headed downtown to a jewelry store. She quickly found exactly what she wanted.

"I'll take those two plain gold wedding bands," she told the saleswoman. "Don't wrap them. Here's my credit card."

The saleswoman was pleased with the direct manner of Bea and the fast sale. "Anything else I can help you with?"

"No, that'll do it. Thanks for your help and courtesy," Bea said.

"No problem." The saleswoman looked around to make sure there were no other customers inside or other salespeople in sight. "Say, are you busy tonight?" Bea smiled at the brashness of a woman who had just sold her two wedding bands, apparently oblivious to or ignoring the fact that Bea must have someone significant in her life and the great likelihood it was a man.

Bea thought about the offer for a second, then smiled sweetly and said, "Sorry, I can't make it tonight."

"Can't blame a girl for trying, can you?" the saleswoman offered.

Bea looked around, moved toward the saleswoman and French-kissed her. "Sure can't." With that she winked and walked out the door.

Bea whistled as she walked up the street clutching the small case with the two wedding rings inside. "That's all there is to it," she said aloud. "When I see Tom next week I'm asking him to marry me."

In his apartment, Phillips sat with his notebook, writing his travel plans:

Day 1. Thursday: Go to Gettysburg, stay the night.

Day 2. Friday: Drive to Cooperstown, stay the night.

Day 3. Saturday: See Baseball Hall of Fame there.

Day 4. Sunday: Drive to Syracuse to see Wilson, stay the night.

Day 5. Monday: Drive to Akron, see Aunt Millie and Uncle Matt, stay the night.

Day 6. Tuesday: Drive to Toledo to see Kate, stay the night.

Days 7 and 8. Wednesday and Thursday: Go to Chicago to see Natalie and Father Luke (hopefully), stay two nights.

Day 9. Friday: Drive to Indiana, see Mom and Dad, stay the night.

Day 10. Saturday: The end, no more nights.

Phillips chewed on the pencil's eraser as he looked over the plans. He smiled in satisfaction. Even for someone who liked planning, it was almost too perfect, but there it was. He would see places he had always wanted to go and spend some time with people whose company he had always loved. The timing would make it a good exit, a perfect exit.

The phone rang.

"Hello"?

"Hi, Tom, it's Bea."

"Hi, Bea. How are you?"

"Fine. And you?"

"Doing good. Just getting ready for my trip back to Indiana."

"Oh, yes, that's coming up, isn't it?"

"Yes."

"How was your trip to Vegas?"

"Good."

"Tom?"

"Yes?"

"Have you given any thought to how you will handle what you talked to me about the other night? I mean, you will need care and home assistance at some point into the future, and surely now you must be getting medical advice."

"I have thought of all those things, and they are being taken care of."

"Is…is there anything I can do to help?"

"Not a thing. Now I really have to get going. I have a lot of things to do to get ready for this trip."

"I understand, Tom…Tom, I love you."

"I'll be seeing you, Bea. Goodbye."

Bea gently hung up the phone, looked away to the wall at a picture she had of the two of them together and cried quietly.

Phillips stared at the phone for a moment after Bea hung up. He started packing, then decided to call Kate.

Kate Phillips was in many ways like her brother. Fiercely independent from her adolescence, she had vowed as a young teenager to never marry, and now in her early 40s had still made good on that pledge. In high school Kate had promised herself she would never be dependent on any man and pushed herself to excel in her studies so that she could support herself. She ended up graduating eighth in her graduating class of 434, went to Notre Dame on a scholarship, got her master's degree at Indiana University in finance and built a highly successful career as an investment banker.

Toledo was not exactly the first place one would think of when mentioning investment banking, but Kate decided early on that she wanted to remain in the Midwest, close to her family. Chicago was too big for her, though she liked visiting it when she wanted some entertainment, relaxation or action, and there was just something about Toledo that appealed to her. And so she had stayed there for more than a decade now, prospering and happy.

Like Phillips, Kate wasn't a great-looking woman, but she had a sexuality that made men notice when she came into a room or walked by or even stood in line at the grocery. Unlike Tom, she wasn't into sports, but instead liked classical music and had played the piano recreationally since learning it during college. Playing the piano filled her heart, relaxed her mind and floated her soul.

Kate dearly loved her brother. They talked on the phone at least every few weeks, always got together when Tom came back to Indiana for a visit and planned to do so again when he came back this July. Mom and Dad had told her of Tom's book. She took great satisfaction in his success with it and loved the book's romance, creativity and racy action. Nobody, not Tom, Mom or Dad, had even a hint of Kate's other side.

Known at home as Kate, she went by Katherine in her professional life and as Katie when she was out to get laid. And the Katie side of Kate loved getting laid, had loved it since she began heavy petting in high school and getting banged regularly while she was in college. After decades of lovemaking, there was only one way to go for her. Foreplay was fine, words of affection were nice, but the guy had to be hung. Indeed, her PC password at work was big, and she meant it.

Kate had her share of men over the years and by now had developed a sense of a man's size that was what you might call unorthodox. She had heard all the theories about race or the size of a man's feet or his hands, but Kate had found over time that the best indicator was the length of a man's last name. Laugh as you will, but it had proven unassailable. She had her share of the Smiths and Joneses, and they were all average, very average. The Sam Adams who did her in the back seat of his van was a joke, and the Martin Eu who boinked her on the beach might just as well have been a sand crab for the dent he put in her snatch. Give her Hans Hausenpfeff, who had poled her on a pile of coats at a holiday party at a friend's house. But most of all give her Pete Kadiddlehopper, a country boy from North

Carolina who played middle linebacker on the Notre Dame football team who took her when he was 22 and she 38. To this day Katie thought wistfully of the night in his apartment when his salami had split her loins sending her into a state of sexual ecstasy unmatched in human history.

At the very least, it felt mighty good.

The phone rang in her office.

"Katherine Phillips speaking."

"Hiya, Kate. It's Tom. Got a sec?"

"Always got a second for you, kid. How are you?"

"Doing well. I won't be long, just wanted to let you know I'll be in town the 11th and hope to see you then or the next day."

"Wouldn't miss it, Tom. You doing well?"

"Yeah. I'm taking my time coming back, taking eight or nine days to see some sights and people along the way. You need anything?"

"Only you, big brother. Mom and Dad miss you, and I do too."

"See you then, Kate. I love you."

"I love you too. Stay well and drive safely. We all need you."

Phillips hung up, feeling a little ashamed. "I have a great sister like this, my parents have always been loving and devoted, and I know all of them would want to help me. And yet I'm pushing them away. Why?"

Yet again, he had no answer. He looked over at the duffel bag where he had packed the gun. Suddenly he felt a need to talk to Natalie. It wasn't that he felt lonely. Phillips knew what it was like to fear – and conquer – the four walls. This was different. Was he confronting his own mortality, really, for the first time?

Aside from Helena, Natalie was the sweetest person who had ever come into his life, and the fact he had fathered her made her more special to him than anyone else in the world. He loved her so. Phillips had no feelings one way or another for her mother, but he had to admit she looked a lot like her. Now 24, Natalie was short at 5 foot 1, had a cute mop of reddish-blonde hair, modest build and a full nose that gave her dark complexion almost a Middle Eastern look.

Phillips thought very infrequently of the night she was conceived. He had met her mother, Sally, a name he had always detested and still did, at a concert. The two of them got stoned, went back to his place and he checked out her yum-yum for half an hour or so. Who could have guessed from such a frivolous encounter such a beautiful creature as Natalie would emerge?

But emerge she did. She lived with her mother, but Phillips visited town regularly, then when he moved to Washington, she took to staying summers with him. He and Sally, despite their indifference to each other, stood together nobly in raising their daughter, who had grown up to be a beautiful young woman, full of life, interests, vibrancy and love for both her mom and dad.

She picked up the phone on the second ring. "Hello?"

"Hi, honey."

"Oh, hi, Daddy. It's wonderful to hear your voice. How are you?"

"Wonderful, now that I'm talking to you. You doing well?"

"Of course. I'm so looking forward to seeing you again. Are you coming through Chicago on your way back to see Mom and Dad?"

"Sure am. I expect to get there on the 12th or 13th. I can drive you back to Indiana with me if you like."

"Let's see, Daddy. I'm off school for a few weeks so I'm working full-time now at the store."

Phillips was very proud of his daughter. From a child's love of animals she had developed into a sensitive young woman committed to their health and well being and was studying to be a veterinarian. Between her work at a pet store, student loans and financial help from her mom and dad, Natalie was doing fine. She was probably most proud of the fact that both had been good parents and neither had strayed from their commitment to her, even though she could never remember a single time that Phillips and Sally had been together, even for a cup of coffee. They had carried any contact necessary to the raising of their daughter either through letters, the phone or e-mail. She was truly beginning to believe her dad when he joked about liking her mother for only the 30 minutes they had spent in an embrace those 24 years ago.

One of the things Phillips liked most about Natalie is that, in her, he saw much of Helena, that perhaps she could have been the daughter he and Helena would have had together had he only seen their love through. From time to time, it was Natalie who made him feel a bit of guilt and remorse about his breakup with Helena because of their similarity and the what-might-have-beens that crossed his mind when he was alone in a park or watching a sunset or walking along a beach.

"How are Grandma and Grandpa?" she asked.

"They're fine, honey, and are really looking forward to seeing you, as am I. Do you need anything from me, money, clothes, whatever?"

"No, Daddy, just bring yourself."

"See you in about a week."

"Till then, Daddy. I love you."

"I love you, sweetheart. Be safe."

Phillips loved everything about his daughter and realized after he hung up that he would miss her dearly after he left. He hoped his death this way would not upset her too deeply, though he admitted to himself that it certainly would. He struggled with these feelings and could not resolve them.

The day had gone quickly, between the phone calls, packing, last-minute details and breaks on the couch with a snack and moments to reflect on what he had done with his years, the good things he would be able to do on his trip back to Indiana and the way he would end his life. It all seemed kind of a dream, this notion of killing himself, but the increasing lapses of forgetfulness and the prospect of being a helpless invalid were more than he thought he could bear, even with the pain it would cause his beloved family and friends.

"Enough," Phillips said as evening descended. Enough putting his mind on overload. Fortified with a meal of ramen mixed with pork and beans, one of his favorite quickies, he sat and watched some baseball, then took care of last-minute details. He tidied up the apartment, checked to see the note to his landlord was where he wanted it to be, made sure he had packed everything he wanted, including the card from Helena, went over the travel plans again and wrote a note to the one woman he wished he had married.

Dear Helena:

When you read this, I will be dead. I am sure you heard of my suicide by now, probably from my mom, but maybe from Bea. I apologize for any pain I have caused from this, but believe me, my beloved friend, I thought of every way I could to avoid this and came up with no solutions.

I am not sure how or what I will tell my mom and dad by way of a farewell note. Just in case I can't find the words for them, I want you to know that I did this because I found out recently I have Alzheimer's disease. I realize there are new drugs and treatments out there to help with the symptoms and effects, and more may develop over the years. And yet, I could not stand the idea of knowing I would slowly lose my capacities and end up being an invalid and dependent on those who should be spared having to care for someone no longer able to care for himself. I like to think I would have been selfish to stay and impose these burdens on others. But I realize I may have been selfish for leaving and robbing those who love me of my being with them. I will never know the answer to this. Perhaps there is no answer.

As I think about my life, I have had many joys, and one of them was my time with you and our continued friendship after our romance ended. But one of the greatest sadnesses I will take with me was that I failed to try to keep our love alive, that I ran from you when I should have embraced you. Please forgive my weakness and lack of courage. Wherever I am now in the hereafter I will be thinking of you.

I love you.

Tom

Phillips re-read the note, liked it, printed it out from his PC, put it in an envelope and packed it, intending to mail it the morning of the 15th, his last morning. The plan, however frightening, still felt good.

It was time to turn in. Phillips read from his novel and Bible, opened his notebook and wrote:

Wednesday, July 5

I will miss this, but I am ready.

Phillips turned off the light and went to sleep.

CHAPTER 14

On the Road

Phillips planned to make this trip and the last days of his life as pleasant as possible. He arose at 8, had a fortifying breakfast, packed his car, took one last look around his apartment and was gone by 10, still plenty of time for the 80-mile drive to Gettysburg but late enough that he managed to avoid the morning rush hour.

He wound down the windows and felt the wind on his face as he headed north on the interstate. How life had changed in just a little over a week. What had been planned as a happy visit back to see Mom and Dad, Natalie and Kate was now to be a death march. Even Phillips had to laugh at that sinister thought as he saw families driving on the highway along with him. Moms and dads and kids headed out for some summer fun and memories that hopefully would stand the test of time, photographs that would later collect dust and weather in a shoebox in a closet corner, children who would grow old and watch their parents age and die and who themselves would age so that no one would ever believe they were once children. When Phillips saw someone living on the streets or lying in a hospital or penned up in a nursing home, he often would tell himself that these people were once children too, full of life and dreams and hope, just as he once had been.

Finally Phillips resolved not to let negative thinking ruin this trip, at least as much as he could help it. He had made his decision and that was that. It was time to forget aging and sorrow and Alzheimer's and all the other shit that happened to people, not just to Tom Phillips, and enjoy. And so he would.

As an avid reader of books about American history, Phillips had been fascinated for many years about the Civil War. One place he had always wanted to visit was Gettysburg, scene of the horrific battle between North and South and by some accounts the turning point in the war. As Phillips drove through the streets of the town, he was fascinated by the fact that the battle had been fought just 137 years ago, which to him seemed like a mere drop in the bucket of time. And yet in terms of life in America, it was an eternity ago. Men marching through dusty streets and along dusty roads in this very place he now stood. Phillips couldn't wait to soak in the sights and sounds. But history would have to wait. Phillips was hungry.

On his way into town Phillips had spotted a Big Boy restaurant, and he headed to it now. You've heard of comfort food. For Phillips this was a comfort restaurant. Throughout his childhood, whenever he and his family headed out for dinner, it was almost invariably to a Big Boy. As Phillips pulled into the parking lot, he wondered if they looked, smelled and felt the same as they had when he was a boy and going out to eat was not only a big deal but also a time of contentment and happiness that he would carry with him into adulthood.

When he stepped inside, he wasn't disappointed. The booths, the smells, the menus, all were just as if he were 9 years old again. Phillips was almost giddy when he sat down and ordered. "What'll it be, hon?" the burly waitress asked him with a plastic smile. Phillips smiled back. "How are you doing today?" he asked. "Just great. What can I get you?" she growled.

Phillips ordered a bowl of chili, half-pound hamburger with a slice of onion and extra dill pickles, a glass of iced tea and a piece of coconut cream pie. After it arrived and as he spread on the yellow mustard, he desperately wanted to call over his waitress and tell her, "This looks so good I'm getting an erection." But Phillips thought better of it lest his life be ended here and now in a Big Boy restaurant far from home, and so he merely said, "Looks good."

Phillips savored every bite of the meal as he ate slowly while reading the local newspaper. Lunch done, he checked into his motel, napped, then went out to see the battlefield he had read so much about.

Three hours later as the guided tour finished up, Phillips sat under a tree and took out his notebook, glad he had brought it along in a small carrying bag. Phillips looked up at the early-evening sun and decided he was ashamed of himself as he began to write.

> *Thursday, July 6, late afternoon, Gettysburg, Pa., battlefield*
> *I'd always wanted to come here and now I'm ashamed I did. How can anybody glorify the death and destruction that happened here? The weekend warriors put on their blue and gray and play at a battle, and that's all they just do is play, with no idea of what it must have been like. They're just like me — it's all a game, and when it came to the real thing we'd probably fail utterly or wonder how anybody could want to make believe they were in a place no one in a sane mind would ever want to be. Even if I lived another 100 years I would never come back here, or for that matter, ever go to a Civil War battlefield again, unless it was to acknowledge the sacrifice that happened there. And even then, the ghosts of the soldiers from these battles would probably want me to just stay the hell away. God, we high and mighty fools of the 21st century are full of shit. How often do we dream of going to a place, then get there and it's a letdown or nothing like we expected?*

Phillips slammed his notebook shut, angry with himself for making what was really no more than a jaunt to such a place where tens of thousands were killed, maimed or left missing. "I want to get out of here," he told himself while returning to his motel room. Phillips showered, found a flyer for a pizza restaurant nearby and prepared to go there for dinner, but first decided to call Mom and Dad. And it was a good thing he has brought along his notebook with phone numbers in it because for the life of him, Phillips couldn't remember the number back at their home in Indiana even though he had called it hundreds of times from memory. "One thing I won't miss, being a forgetful old turd." He gave his notebook the finger as he looked at the number.

But then Phillips smiled as he took out his cell phone, a gift to himself just before he left Washington. "Am I becoming a dot-comer?" he said with a chuckle as he picked up the phone. He had to admit it was convenient, and with the service plans offered it was actually cheaper when calling long-distance. Phillips thought of Michael Smithson and their Las Vegas talk and wondered how he and his mom were faring, just as Peggy picked up the phone in Indiana.

"Hello?"

"Hi, Mom. Just wanted to say hello and see how you and Dad are doing."

"We're wonderful, honey. Both of us just can't wait to see you."

"I can't wait to see you either, Mom. I'm figuring on getting there sometime on Friday the 14th. I'm taking my time coming back, and I even was hoping to see Uncle Matt and Aunt Millie on the way there."

"Tommy, that would be wonderful. I'm sure they would be delighted to see you even though it has been so many years since you last talked. Here's their phone number."

Phillips wrote it down and wondered what his parents could possibly say to him if they knew what his plan was once he got back. Then he quickly put it out of his mind because he knew what he was going to do

would hurt them terribly, and the thought of hurting these two good people was something he could not bear.

"Thanks, Mom. I'll see you soon. Say hi to Dad."

"I will. Your father said to be sure to say hi when you called. We both
love you, Tommy."

"I love you too, Mom. Bye."

"Bye."

After dinner Phillips enjoyed a leisurely walk through town window
shopping and enjoying the serenity of a small city on a summer evening.
Phillips wondered what it was like to live in Gettysburg. He envied those
who had lives and families and commitments, then caught himself that
maybe they, too, lived lives of desperation and envied a traveler from
Washington who came to town to look at the battle site and returned to
his exciting life in the city.

Just in case, Phillips had written the directions from his motel to the
restaurant in case his mind lapsed again, but he made it back fine and settled into his room for the night to watch *Austin Powers: The Spy Who
Shagged Me* on HBO. After watching awhile, all that talk of shagging
made him want to do some himself, and he thought of trying his luck in a
local bar. "After all, I never have poked a woman from Pennsylvania,"
Phillips said aloud as he wrestled with his shag-or-not-to-shag dilemma.
Comfort finally won out over his stirrings so Phillips retired to the can for
a quickie with Miss Five, returned to his movie, then peacefully went to
sleep. He slept soundly.

Helena had awakened Thursday feeling unsettled, and it stayed with
her into the afternoon. Finally she called Bea.

"Hi, Bea. This is Helena. Got a second?"

"Of course. What's up?"

"I've been thinking about Sand..., uh, I mean Tom. In fact, I can't get
this out of my mind. Can we meet after work?"

"Helena, I know how you feel. Sure, let's meet at Max's, just up the
street from where I work. You know the place, right?"

"I do, Bea. See you there."

Two hours later the two women met over drinks to discuss their mutual friend, hoping to find a way to deal with his problem as they each wrestled with their emotional disquiet. Neither said anything for a time. Helena sipped a gin and tonic while Bea swirled the wine in her glass as she looked absently at her uneaten salad. Finally Bea spoke. "Helena, I've told you before about my love for Tom, but I'm thinking I have to do more than just profess an empty emotion."

"I don't think saying you love someone is an empty emotion, Bea," Helena answered as she stared intently at her.

"You know what I mean. Here I am telling you that I love Tom, and I'm not doing anything about it."

"Have you told him?"

"Yes, I did, on the phone yesterday, but he just dismissed it."

"I don't think you should push him."

"Maybe not, but I don't believe he's thinking clearly now. I'm worried about him."

"Tom is a grown man. He will know what to do."

"Maybe, but I don't want to take any chances. When I go back to visit him and his folks, I'm going to ask Tom to marry me."

Helena looked outside. A couple walked hand in hand, reminding her of when she and Tom used to walk like that, window shopping on their way to lunch or dinner. She wondered now whether she was challenging Bea out of Tom's interest or her own. "Silly thoughts," she said to herself and looked down.

"What?" Bea asked.

"Nothing, just talking to myself. If you think asking Tom to marry you will be good for the both of you, then I think you should. But be careful. Believe me, I know Tom. Once he thinks someone is getting too close, he backs off."

"Is that what happened with the two of you?"

Helena fought back tears. "Yes."

"You still love him, don't you?"

"Bea, I never stopped. But that's not the issue now, is it?"

Phillips woke early Friday, eager for the day ahead. He had a five-hour drive to Cooperstown and wanted to get there by late afternoon and still be able to relax and enjoy the drive through the Pennsylvania and New York countryside.

Breakfast was grand. Three eggs over easy, rye toast, hash browns, four slices of bacon, orange juice and coffee. "Man, maybe I'll just eat myself to death," he said as he took the first mouthful. Phillips savored his meal while he alternately read the morning newspaper and looked out the window as the town came to life. People going to work, tourists wandering onto the streets, children at play. Life uncomplicated, just as Phillips liked it.

After breakfast, Phillips walked across the street to a park, found a bench and called his aunt and uncle on the cell phone.

A man answered.

"Hello, Uncle Milt?"

"Who is this?" the man answered gruffly.

"This is Tom, Tom Phillips, your nephew. My folks are Joe and Peggy Phillips."

"Tom…my word, hello, Tom. Gosh, we haven't talked in years. How are you?"

"I know it's been a long time. Uncle Milt, I am driving back to visit my parents and will be driving through Akron next Monday and thought maybe I would stop to say hi to you and Aunt Millie."

There was silence for a few seconds. Then Milt spoke. "I…I'd sure love to see you, Tom. I can't be sure your Aunt Millie will be here but make sure to stop by anyway. Let me give you the directions."

Phillips wrote down the way to get there, said his goodbyes and hung up. Something seemed to be bothering his uncle, but Phillips couldn't say why he thought so. "Maybe it's just me," he said, got up from the bench, took a deep breath of the morning air and headed to his car for the drive north to Cooperstown.

The trip was glorious. If he could have bottled the serenity on his drive along the quiet roads through tranquil countryside he would have made a mint. As it was, Phillips arrived in Cooperstown feeling like a millionaire, all of his cares having subsided somewhere along the 280-mile drive from Gettysburg. He found a motel in town, went out to dinner topped off by an ice cream cone and a leisurely walk back to his room and turned in early.

Helena didn't know what to think on her way back home after meeting with Bea. She only knew she had to quiet these feelings for Phillips that she thought she had put away but now realized she hadn't after all. Thomas was waiting for her when she returned.

"Hi, love. Anything going on?"

"What do you mean?"

"You have just seemed a little preoccupied lately, and now you were out seeing Bea again. I know you're friends, but twice in a few days is a bit more than normal."

"Thomas…I, I just can't say anything right now."

He caught her as she tried to walk past, put his hands on her shoulders and held her at arm's length. Thomas gazed at her, nudging her eyes back to his when she tried to look away.

"Whatever it is that is bothering you, I am here. I know it can't possibly be something I have done because I have done nothing more than love you with all my heart. I will do that until death us do part. I don't know what is going on inside you now, nor do I ask you to tell me. All I ask is that you love me back as I love you."

Helena looked at her husband, admiring his strength, drawing from his love, absorbing his peace and strong sense of self. She took him by the hand onto the patio, where she told him about the events of her, Bea and Phillips.

Phillips took out his notebook again.

Friday, July 7, Cooperstown
I can't remember feeling this content. If I died in my sleep tonight
there would be no regrets. That would free me from what I know I
have to do, but I suppose that would be too easy. Now I know how
Father Luke feels, happy with himself and his life. If only … Ah,
screw it. Good night to myself.

Phillips arrived at the Baseball Hall of Fame the next morning when the doors opened and spent the day there in awe of the greats who had played the game. Phillips had loved baseball since he was 7 and played in his first Little League game, and his appreciation for the game had only grown as the years went on. Now here he was, in the spiritual presence of those who had excelled at it. Babe Ruth, Hank Aaron, Jackie Robinson, Stan Musial, Lou Gehrig. Some of these men he had seen play, others he had read about. He couldn't get enough of this place and stayed until the doors closed for the day.

"I wonder if Wilson has seen this," Phillips thought to himself as he walked out. He took out his phone while walking back to his motel and dialed his friend. Could it really be over 25 years since he and Wilson had first met?

Wilson picked up the phone on the second ring. "Hullo."

"Hey, Wilson, it's me, Tom. How you doin'?"

"Tom who?"

"Tom Phillips, man."

"Tom Phillips? For real?"

"In the flesh, my friend. It's been awhile."

It had been awhile indeed. The two always exchanged Christmas cards and an occasional postcard but hadn't talked on the phone for at least half a dozen years and hadn't seen each for probably 10.

"It sure has been awhile, Tom. What's up?"

"Actually I'm kind of in your neighborhood. I'm in Cooperstown on my way back to visit my folks and was thinking I'd like to visit you if that'd be alright."

"Alright? Of course it would! Too bad you didn't call earlier. I could've met you down there."

Phillips felt a little guilty for not having told his friend so they could have spent the day together and caught up on old times. But there would be time for that now when he visited.

"You still at the same address in Syracuse, Wilson?"

"I surely am. Let me give you directions. When are you coming?"

"I figured I'd get there tomorrow around noon and maybe stay the afternoon."

"Hey, plan on staying the night. I've got plenty of room."

"Won't Joanie mind?"

"Joanie's gone, Tom."

"Gone? When?"

"Five years already."

"Man, why didn't you tell me? Shit, all these years you've signed your cards Will and Joanie and she was gone?"

"I didn't have the heart to tell you, man. But let's not get into that. Looking forward to seeing you again. I'll make some barbecue and we'll have some fun."

"Deal, my friend. See you tomorrow."

"Drive safely, Tommy."

As Phillips returned to his motel, he was still trying to digest the news about the breakup of Wilson's marriage. He remembered when Wilson met Joanie that summer he and his friend had played minor league baseball together, a shining time in both of their lives. But what shocked him even more was that Wilson had not breathed a word of it to him for five years. What misery must the man have gone through, Phillips asked himself.

After a shower and halfheartedly watching a movie, Phillips turned in. He opened his Bible and read the passage from Timothy that Father Luke liked so much. ...I have finished the race, I have kept the faith... Phillips closed the book. "How I wish I could say those words to myself and know they were true."

CHAPTER 15

▼

WILSON

Phillips headed north, picked up the interstate and drove west toward Syracuse. Lost in thought about the breakup of Wilson's marriage, he took little notice of the countryside bathed in summer sun on a lazy Sunday morning. Life was all around him. Farmers, townspeople, children, adults, babies, dogs, cats, birds going about their business. A drop of water on a leaf reflecting the sunlight in a tiny rainbow. A ladybug landing on his windshield, then gone in search of a new adventure. The gentle touch of a breeze, like the flutter of an angel's wing.

Phillips saw and felt none of them. And his concern about Wilson brought him back to his own problems. He asked himself he if was over-reacting to his friend's situation. He knew of guys who pretended for the world to see that they were sad when in reality things couldn't have been better. The aggrieved husband as martyr. Hell, he knew of guys who had played on their make-believe misery to get laid by comforting female friends. One he knew, Sam Ehren, had bedded his ex-wife's sister on just such a pretense.

"Maybe it's all just bullshit about Wilson's wife going. Maybe he's really happy. Maybe my own misery is just a bunch of horseshit too. Who knows?" Phillips was talking to himself by the time he was ready to leave the highway and head for Wilson's house. "First sign of madness? It doesn't really matter, does it?"

Before he knew it, Phillips was pulling up in front of Wilson's house, a modest yellow bungalow on a quiet street in a corner of the world in Syracuse, New York. Phillips was surprised to see Wilson had filled his front yard with flowers of every color and at least a dozen varieties, something he wouldn't have guessed about him.

The two would become unlikely friends then, that summer they met, Phillips a 21-year-old college graduate from a small-city upbringing, Wilson a street-wise 19-year-old black from Savannah, Georgia. Yet there they were in 1973, fate bringing them together in Bluefield, West Virginia, to play professional baseball in the Appalachian League. Both had a dream of rising to play Major League baseball, and both had about the same chance of making it. Beyond that they had nothing in common. And that, perhaps, was their bond.

Phillips felt almost like he was sleepwalking as he walked toward the house and rang the doorbell, and then suddenly Wilson was there. "Will, great to see you again," Phillips said as he pumped his friend's hand. Wilson returned the handshake firmly. "Tom, nice to see you too. Please, come in."

As he shook Wilson's hand, then embraced him, it seemed like only a short time ago that they had shaken hands for the first time in the dugout at the Bluefield stadium. Now, as then, a point of pride for both men was that they had played the game. No matter where life would take him, Phillips had told himself as he packed his duffel bag for the last time and left the ballpark when he was cut later that summer of '73, he would look back and be happy for this. He thought of that in the doorway of Wilson's house, a long way from Bluefield, West Virginia, for both of them.

"You're looking good," Phillips said as Wilson ushered him into the house and took his bag. And he honestly meant it. The years had been kind to his friend. There was a touch of gray on his temples now, but he had kept the muscular build that had made him a power hitter in the minor leagues and carried him much closer to the Major Leagues than Phillips. In fact, Wilson had advanced to Triple-A in Rochester, New York, just one rung below the Show. His dream died just as Phillips' had; it had just taken another couple of years to do so.

"So are you, my friend," Wilson said, and he meant it as well, save for a touch of sadness he noticed in Phillips' eyes that hadn't been there when they first met. Then again, maybe Phillips' eyes had seen more over the years and weren't sad so much as they were simply older. He couldn't tell. "Let's bring your suitcase to the guest room. Take some time to freshen up and rest if you want, then we'll catch up on old times."

"Deal."

The simple touches of Wilson's house impressed Phillips. He could have lived there himself, changing very little. Phillips looked around the living room. A ballgame was on TV. "Still like the game, eh, Will?"

"I've never stopped loving it, Tom. Have you?"

"Not one bit."

Wilson led him down the hall. "I'll let you put your things down and relax. You'll find me outside. I've started a fire so we can have ourselves a barbecue and drink some beer."

"Sounds fine, Will."

Phillips looked around the room, comfortably furnished and bright, lit up by the midday sun that poured through a window past open drapes. It was the photograph on the wall that stopped him. There stood Wilson and Joanie in a picture from their wedding day. Standing among the friends and family joining them in the photograph was Phillips himself. He couldn't believe it, walked over to the picture and ran his finger across it, stopping on the person he once was. He couldn't remember ever having seen this picture before and perhaps the only thing that stunned him more than finding out about it was that Wilson would keep it on the wall when the dreams and love captured on film had died years before. It felt to him like keeping a picture of your dead mother or father taken in their casket.

He washed his face, looked at his reflection in the mirror and went downstairs. He found Wilson in the backyard drinking a beer and cooking two rib eye steaks, half a dozen sausages and four hamburgers on the grill. Phillips sat across from him at a redwood picnic table.

"You expecting company, Will?"

"No, company's here. You and I have a lot to talk about it, and we can't do it on empty stomachs."

Phillips cracked open a can of beer and touched Wilson's lightly. "Salute."

"Salute, Tom."

Phillips looked at the trees reaching to the sky from Wilson's and his neighbors' yards. This place had a sense of permanence to it, a feeling of belonging. Like the trees, Wilson had put down his roots. It showed in his demeanor, in the way he had put his household together. Still, Phillips was bothered by the fact his friend was now going through life by himself, his partner gone.

"Say, Will, I had never seen that picture before, the one from your wedding day that had me in it. Or did you show me one and I just forgot about it?"

"No, Tom. I doubt you had seen it. After the wedding you left town and I don't believe we'd ever have had occasion since for you to look at it."

"If you don't mind my asking, why do you keep that picture?"

"It was a happy day, one of the happiest of my life. Because my marriage ended doesn't diminish the beauty of my wedding day."

"Doesn't it hurt?"

"The hurt is long gone. I keep pictures of myself from our playing days down in Bluefield too. I can't play ball anymore, but that doesn't take away from that time, does it?

"Now that I can think about it, Joanie leaving me almost was funny in some ways."

"Funny?"

"Yeah. Remember that shit we heard in high school when a girl broke up with us and said 'It's not you, it's me'?"

"Don't tell me that's what Joanie said to you."

"Gospel truth," Wilson said and laughed. "Can you believe that shit?"

""What do you suppose is the real reason?"

"Tom, I have no idea. To this day I have never found out. After she moved out I never saw her again."

"Were you good to her?"

"I tried, but as I look back on it, I could've been better. I think that's true of anyone, don't you suppose?"

"I don't know, Will."

"All I know is that I didn't mistreat her or run around on her. I was faithful and dutiful. Sometimes that isn't enough. I don't begrudge her leaving, not any more. Some people can't be happy with other people. I just hope she has found what I have."

"What's that?"

"Peace of mind."

The flames flared on the barbecue. Wilson went to sprinkle some water on the fire, turned the meat, took another couple of beers from the ice chest in the yard and sat across from Tom again. He looked with sincerity into his friend's eyes.

"How about you, Tom? You ever get married?"

"Nope. Just never met the right woman."

Phillips thought to himself, told himself that if he and Helena had married, there never would have been a breakup like with Wilson and Joanie. His thoughts drifted to Helena, then to Bea.

"Humph."

"What did you say, Tom?"

"Oh, nothing. Just was thinking about somebody and it felt strange. Do you ever hear from the guys we played with back in Bluefield?"

"I heard from a few for awhile, but then like the others they became gofers or disappeared into the corporate ether. You?"

"No, I never heard from any of them."

"Do you ever hear from Betty?"

Both men laughed. Neither talked as both looked off in different directions, Wilson at the clouds, Phillips at the methodical drip, drip, drip from a garden hose, its work for the day now done.

Betty. She was a standing joke between Phillips and Wilson whenever they met, no matter how many years had elapsed. And yet for both, she was someone, something linking them to a past both treasured.

As Phillips looked off at the trees, he could still feel that night those many years ago.

He and Wilson were on the team in Bluefield, Wilson a power-hitting right fielder, Phillips a slick batsman and gifted fielder who played second base, two men who had found each other and were cementing a friendship through the simple act of chatting as they ran out to their positions on the field each night. On a sticky Tuesday evening in late June, Wilson noticed her first, a blonde sitting two rows behind their dugout who had a pair of jugs that could suffocate a man if he wasn't careful. Wilson had gotten around with women for several years now and could spot one on the make from a block away.

Wilson watched her follow Phillips with her eyes as he took the field at the bottom of the second inning, and then again when he returned to the dugout afterward.

"As we run out on the field after our turn at bat, check out the blonde behind our dugout. She's eyeing you."

"Bullshit."

"Bullshit, my ass. Check her out."

When Phillips returned to his position, he looked and there she was. And Wilson was right. She most definitely was looking at him.

When Phillips came to bat in the fifth inning, he poked an opposite-field double down the right field line. As he stood on second base dusting off his pants after sliding in safely, there she was, clapping and jumping up and down, her boobs bouncing like a couple of cantaloupes stuck in the top of her yellow summer dress.

Wilson ran alongside Phillips when it was Bluefield's turn to return to the field. He leaned over to him and said almost like an order, "You've got a piece of ass waiting for you in the stands, now don't blow it."

Phillips laughed as he got to his position and turned to face the field. His erection tugged at his jockstrap, and he hoped for all the world none of his teammates would notice.

She was waiting at the players' entrance after the game, walked up to Phillips and Wilson as they left the stadium and put a piece of paper in his face. "May I have your autograph?" Her sweet Southern accent dripped in the humid night air.

Wilson clapped his friend on the back. "Gotta go, my man. See you here tomorrow."

Phillips watched him walk away.

"Well?" came the sweet Southern accent.

"Well, what?"

"May I have your autograph?"

"Oh, sure. What's your name?"

"Betty."

"Just Betty?"

"Yes, just Betty. I know your name. It's Tom Phillips. I like the way you play."

Phillips blushed and felt his dick harden again. He took the paper, signed his name, then handed it and the pen back to her.

Betty and Phillips walked up the street and around a corner, talking about baseball, the weather, this and that.

By the time they reached a small coffee shop three blocks from the park Betty had locked her right arm in Phillips' left. Her pink lipstick and sweet but not overpowering perfume made her seem almost girlish in an endearing way to Phillips. He looked at Betty while they ate and talked. She was sexy, had a strong build, full face with a touch of freckles and blonde hair that just reached the neckline of her dress. Up close, her cans were even more spectacular than they had appeared from his perch on the infield dirt. They both ordered a third beer and took them along as they left the restaurant.

"Do you live around here?" Phillips asked.

"Nope, do you?"

"Well my place is a few miles away and …"

"Actually, Tom, I was wondering if we could return to the ballpark."

"The ballpark?"

"Yes. I've never been in one with everybody else gone. Do you know a way in?"

Betty giggled.

"Sure, follow me."

They walked back to the park. Phillips found the opening near the right-field foul line.

"They keep this here for the grounds crew so they don't have to walk all the way to the entrance to get inside," Phillips tried to explain, but Betty had already gone ahead. She was waiting for him, the outfield grass damp from the evening mist, smelling fresh like the first scent of spring after the winter snow.

Betty turned to face him, took a strap in each hand and dropped her dress to the ground. She stepped out of it and removed her bra just as she reached Phillips, who cupped her tits and kissed her deeply. Betty undid his trousers, sank to her knees and took him in her mouth. Just as he gasped, she laid down on the ground and opened her legs.

"Betty," Phillips croaked, went to his knees, pulled off her panties and clumsily jumped on her.

"Whoa there, cowboy," Betty whispered. "Do you think you're digging for oil? You don't go straight down from the top, you push yourself inside from underneath, see?"

She opened wider to show him her pink.

"You almost act as if you …"

Phillips looked at her without saying anything.

"Oh, my God, Tom, is this your first time?"

Phillips looked away.

"Yes," he said quietly.

"Tom, I'm so sorry if I embarrassed you. Let me show you."

The two of them knelt on the grass, the stars shining brightly above, and kissed gently, then more fervently. She gently rolled Phillips onto his back, mounted him and showed him the way.

After his sexual baptism, the two laid together holding hands and looking up at the sky.

"Will I see you again?" Phillips asked.

"No, Tom."

He balanced himself on his arm.

"Why not?"

"I'm just passing through, taking a trip on my summer break. I'll be gone in the morning."

"Where do you live?"

"Oklahoma."

"What do you do?"

"I'm a second-grade teacher."

"You're a teacher?"

"Sure. You seem surprised. What, you don't think teachers like to fuck?"

"Of course, but …"

"But nothing, now shush." She put her index finger to his lips, kissed him on the cheek and got dressed. They walked out, hand in hand, through the opening in the fence. Betty turned to face Phillips.

"Goodbye, Tom. Have a happy life." Phillips watched as she walked into the night, straining to see her, and then she was gone.

Betty was right. Phillips never had seen her again.

"Hey, Tom, yo, Tom. You there?"

Phillips looked over. Wilson was talking, pushing a can of beer toward him. "That was some daydream you had. It was like you were in another world."

Phillips snapped back to reality, to Wilson's house, to his own one-way trip back to where he had started.

"Sorry, I was just thinking about Betty. She was a nice lady."

Wilson winked. "I'm sure she was."

Phillips took a drink of beer and looked at a bird that landed on a clothesline in a neighbor's yard. "You heard about this new football league, Tom?"

"Yeah, you mean the XFL?"

"That's it. I have this idea. You know how they say they want to make it bold and flashy and sexy? What do you think of this? Every game one of the cheerleaders wears no panties, but nobody knows which. The people in the stands have to keep watching until they spot her and hope she does enough splits and leg kicks to show them something. Nifty idea, huh?"

"You're a sick man, my friend, as crazy as when we played ball together."

"Not totally, but I surely hope I never become a stick in the mud."

"What do you do for a living nowadays anyway?"

"Believe it or not, I'm a high school math teacher. I went back to school and got my teaching degree and have been teaching for nearly three years now."

"And you like it?"

"I like it a lot. It's a responsible job, I coach the baseball team, and I've always liked working with kids."

"Do you get any young pussy?"

Wilson laughed a deep, throaty sound. "Man, I'm too old for that shit, and I don't want the trouble, know what I mean?"

"I do."

The two friends talked on about their lives after baseball as young men, about opportunities lost and gained, until finally they were talked out. They laid on the grass and gently fell asleep, the afternoon sun warming their faces as they napped.

They awoke in the evening, the setting sun putting a warm, orange glow on the day the two of them had spent together. Finally Phillips sat up and spoke.

"Wilson, you seem to have it together even with Joanie gone. I know how much much you loved her. How do you keep going on? What stops you from just giving up?"

Wilson stayed on his back for a moment looking up at the sky, then sat up beside Phillips. "I guess...I believe it's because I don't dwell on the past or look too far to the future. I just try to take life in bite-sized chunks, and so far it seems to be working."

Phillips was thinking on this when Wilson spoke again.

"You know what I still miss about baseball?"

"What's that, Will?"

"The sweet smell of that outfield grass, pure and unspoiled. I can breathe it in now and feel like it was only yesterday that we were there, sharing it together."

Phillips looked over at him and extended his hand. Wilson shook it warmly. In the distance, crickets sang. The night fell.

CHAPTER 16

GETTING CLOSER

Monday, July 10

Man, it's good to see Wilson again. I envy him, surviving hardship and being happy, when I feel so inadequate, so unsure of myself. I can't shake these spasms of forgetfulness, which I know are just the prelude to something far worse. It seems funny, me having only five days to live. I wonder if this is how the poor buggers on Death Row feel. Maybe I should pick a last meal for myself; God, I am a morose bastard. As I think about it I don't know how anyone will possibly be able to understand why I killed myself. Even I have a hard time understanding it, comprehending what I am planning to do, and yet it seemed right at the time and so it must be the right thing to do. Trust your instincts. Isn't that what Helena always told me? But didn't she also say when in doubt, don't? I don't think I am doubting myself, do you?

Phillips wanted to write more, felt the need to write more to deal with his fears, but he had to get going. He wanted to be on the road by 9. It was already 7 a.m., he had to say goodbye to Wilson before heading to Akron to see his aunt and uncle, and the drive there would take about six hours.

As he swung his feet onto the floor and prepared to get up, the smell of bacon and eggs floated into his room from the kitchen. He could hear Wilson singing. "Take me out to the ballgame, take me out to the crowd. Buy me some peanuts and a bottle of beer, I don't care if my ass ever is here…" Phillips laughed so loud Wilson could hear him and stopped his singing.

"Hey, man, don't you like my personal touch to the song?"

"I love it," Phillips shouted through the door. He was smiling as he took his shower. The memory of yesterday with shared thoughts and good times with Wilson warmed him. He was glad he had stopped off to see him.

Packed and ready to go, he went to the kitchen and gave Wilson a clap on the back as his friend brought the food to the table. "Better hurry, it's gonna get cold."

The two ate in silence for a few minutes. "Where are you off to?" Wilson asked.

"I'm heading to Akron to see an aunt and uncle I haven't seen in years, going to Toledo to see my sister, then to Chicago for a day before I get to Indiana to see my folks."

"Sure wish you could stay longer. School's out so I have plenty of time to watch the game and just hang around. It'd be good to spend more time together." Wilson looked at Phillips, searching him with his eyes. "I never lack for company, but it sure is nice seeing you again."

Phillips wanted to confide in Wilson, wanted to tell him everything about his journey back to Indiana for the last time, to say a final goodbye. "Wish I could, Will, but I've got to get going," he said finally.

"I know," Wilson said, a tinge of sadness to his voice.

As Wilson cleared the table, Phillips went back to his room to get his things and call ahead to Akron to let them know he was coming. A woman answered on the second ring, as if she was expecting a call.

"Hello?"

"Hi, this is Tom Phillips. Is that you Aunt Millie?"

She was silent for a few seconds. "Oh…yes, it's me, Millie. Who is this again?"

"It's Tom, Tom Phillips, your nephew."

"Tom! Yes, of course. Matt said you were going to visit us. When are you coming?"

"I was hoping to stop there today. Maybe we could go out to dinner, the three of us?"

"I won't hear of it. Matt had said he wanted to make you some of his famous hamburgers when you came to town, and we had hoped our children Howard and Leslie would come by as well to see you. You will be staying the night, won't you?"

"Actually I was figuring I would find a motel nearby and hoped you could recommend one."

"Motel. Nonsense. You're staying with us, and that's final."

"Well, if you insist, Aunt Millie. I figure I'll be there about 3 if that is all right."

"Absolutely. It will be so nice to see you again. It has been too many years."

"I'll see all of you soon. Looking forward to it."

Phillips hung up after getting directions to their house from the highway. There was something about his aunt's voice that stayed with him, an affectatious way of trying to sound young for a woman who had to be in her mid-60s at least. Not that there was anything wrong with staying zestful, but there also was something to be said for acting your age. "Show a little dignity," is how his dad had always put it. Phillips shrugged.

Hey, I'll only be there a few hours, and besides, I'll get some of Uncle Matt's burgers again. Phillips smiled when he recalled family get-togethers with his aunt and uncle and their two kids, how Howard and Leslie kept bopping each other like any other brother and sister, and how his uncle could make such special grilled hamburgers. It might have been the way he marinated them, or peppered them or cooked them or a combination of all three. Whatever, Phillips couldn't recall ever having had better.

Wilson was waiting outside on the front porch as Phillips came from the bedroom with his bag. "Here, I made you a couple of bacon and egg sandwiches on rye. You still like them with mayo and a touch of lettuce?"

Phillips stared at Wilson, then smiled. "You haven't forgotten a thing, have you?"

"Well, not some things." The two looked at each other, remembering breakfasts of long ago between two friends sharing a dream as young men. They hugged.

"Goodbye, Will."

"Goodbye, Tom."

Phillips drove away. He waved with his left arm out the window until he turned the corner and was away. Wilson stood on his porch, looking in the distance long after Phillips had gone, then turned and went back inside.

As Phillips was heading onto the highway resuming his journey, Helena was meeting Bea over tea and omelets at a D.C. coffee shop.

Helena got quickly to the point.

"Bea, I have talked over our discussion with Thomas, and we both believe it would be good for me to travel to Indiana to help Tom deal with this. What do you think?"

Bea thought for a moment. "My only worry is that we will overwhelm him. I honestly believe he needs all the support he can get at this point, but you know Tom. He's so independent, we might force him into just leaving or telling all of us to go fuck ourselves."

"You do have a point there." Helena smiled. "You and I know a lot about Tom by now. This is all just so sad for him, but surely he isn't the only one who has gotten sick. He's just lucky they found it in time and he can get proper treatment. With all the medical breakthroughs these days, they might even find a cure before it sets in too badly. But somehow I just don't believe he is thinking that way now.

"Bea, Thomas and I had discussed the idea of calling his parents and telling them. What do you think?"

"Bad idea. No way should we lay this on them. If anything's to be done, at least for now, it's up to us to do it."

"You're right of course. You don't think my going is overkill, do you?"

"Who ever heard of overkill on caring?"

Phillips was right on schedule as he headed toward Akron. It was another beautiful Midwest day. Puffs of clouds dotted the soft blue sky. A Reds-Pirates baseball game was on the radio. The drive was peaceful.

Phillips thought of what he would talk about with his aunt, uncle and cousins. He remembered one of their visits to Indiana. He was a teenager at the time, and for days afterward he and Kate had laughed about their Uncle Matt's eating habits. To be unkind about it, he ate like a pig. Even white bread was an adventure for this man who had the miserable habit of always eating with his mouth open so that when he chewed it sounded like a horse clip-clopping on pavement. During a spaghetti dinner at the Phillips' table one night, chunks of noodles and meat shot out of his mouth like confetti. To make matters worse, he smacked his lips, his Adam's apple bobbed like an orange floating on a rippling lake and he drank any beverage so slowly and deliberately you thought he was trying to balance the glass on his lips.

"God," Phillips said as he drove along on the highway, "how could Aunt Millie have stood it all these years? I guess that is what love is all about. Or is it what suffering is all about?"

But Phillips was in no mood to dwell on such weighty subjects so he spent the last 50 miles on the way to Akron fantasizing about Paula Rosenthal in the sack.

Helena, proceeding with her plan, put in a call to Phillips' mom. "Why Helena, what a pleasant surprise." Peggy always was happy to hear from her.

"Hi, Mrs. Phillips. Good to talk to you again. I don't have long to chat now, but I wanted you to know I will be joining you later this week after all."

"That's splendid, honey. I know Joe will be so pleased too. Do you need a place to stay while you're in town? I hope your husband and children can come."

"No, I'm coming alone. It will just be for the weekend. I can find a motel when I arrive."

"Well, whatever suits you. See you this weekend. Have a safe trip."

"See you Saturday. Say hi to Mr. Phillips for me."

Peggy sat on a kitchen chair after saying goodbye to Helena and looked out the window at two sparrows chirping on her clothesline. There was something about Helena's call she found unsettling. It may have been just the unexpected plans of both Bea and Helena to travel to the party at the Phillips' house this weekend. "Why the sudden change of heart?" she asked. No one was there to answer her, and she didn't have an answer herself, but the question nagged at her. If nothing else, she thought it to be a mother's instinct.

Maybe Natalie knew if something was going on.

The phone rang in Natalie's apartment. Peggy hadn't really expected her to be there but at the least she could leave a message. Sure enough, the voicemail clicked in. "Hi, this is Natalie Adams Phillips. I'm not able to take your call at the moment, but if you leave your name and number I'll call you back as soon as I can. Take care. Bye."

Peggy so loved Natalie, who was everything she had always dreamed of in a granddaughter. At first she had been hurt that Natalie's mother and father weren't together and the three of them wouldn't grow together as a family, but after a time Peggy accepted that as just part of a new day and age. To her, Natalie as a child was the image of her own Tommy when he was young, and now that she was a grown-up with her own hopes and dreams, she reminded Peggy of what her son had been like as he set out in the world.

"Natalie, honey, this is Grandma. Could you call me when you have a chance? Nothing urgent. I love you." Peggy lied. A feeling of urgency was coming over her, and she didn't know why. All she knew was that she suddenly was worried for her son.

Natalie got to the phone just as the voicemail ended. After playing back the message, she chuckled as she often did when she heard her greeting. Natalie had taken both of her parents' surnames because there was no reason she had to choose one over the other, and she liked to joke she would probably marry someone named Adamovich so that her name could be Natalie Adams Phillips Adamovich. Phillips, who wasn't particularly fond of the Adams part of her name, but then Sally wasn't that crazy about the Phillips part of it either, would say in all seriousness, "Try signing that on a check. There wouldn't be enough room for you to put your name."

"Oh, Daddy," Natalie would answer, "it's just a joke." When she looked at him then with those girlish dark eyes and dimpled smile, there wasn't a thing in the world Phillips wouldn't do for his daughter. Her charm and engaging manner worried him in a world full of perverts and weirdoes. "You shouldn't put your name on the phone like that. The wrong person could get hold of it."

Her answer was the same every time he tried to hide her bright light. "Fuck 'em." And while he would cringe to hear this once little girl use such language, he could hardly tell her not to since he always used it himself.

Natalie called Peggy right back. "Hi, Grandma. It's me. I just got back as you called. What's up?"

"It's always so nice to hear your voice, honey. I was just wondering if Tom had talked to you lately about anything bothering him."

"No, Grandma. He called a few days ago and sounded fine and was looking forward to his visit this week. He'll be in Chicago in a couple of days, and then of course I'll be seeing him on the weekend at your place. Is anything the matter?"

"No, Natalie, I guess it's just me. Don't give it another thought. I'll see you this weekend. We are looking forward to it."

"I am too, Grandma. See you then. And don't worry. It's bad for your health."

Peggy felt a little better but wasn't sure whether Natalie had genuinely eased her concern or just made her feel good with that endearing manner of hers. "Bye, Natalie. See you soon. I love you."

"I love you, Grandma. Bye."

Phillips drove up to the home in Akron. The neighborhood was upper class, the homes big and impressive. He had no idea his aunt and uncle lived so well though he never had reason to think about it. As he walked up the steps to the house, the front door opened. He was greeted by a trim, short woman with a pixie haircut and beady blue eyes, shirt tied at the midriff and black leotards. A white leather belt circled her waist and held a cell phone by the clip.

"Tom? How nice to see you after all these years," she said and hugged him close. She didn't let go until Phillips stepped back. "Aunt Millie?"

"In the flesh," she answered and winked. "I'm so glad you could stop by to see us."

Phillips could swear his own aunt, his mom's youngest sister, was coming on to him. He couldn't help but notice the watch on her left wrist, a flashy number that looked to be the size of a coffee-cup saucer. Phillips barely stopped from snickering. As he stood there, a booming voice came from around the corner. "Tom, is that you?"

If opposites attract, Matt and Millie Townsend were a match made in heaven. Uncle Matt walked up, a mountain of a man whose hand swallowed Phillips' as if it were a child's. He wore jeans, a plaid shirt and cowboy boots and at Christmas could have passed for Santa Claus by just getting into a red suit.

"Please come in, my boy. Make yourself at home."

The house was gorgeous, the living room furnished with teak and leather and a huge TV. Millie's phone rang. "Karaoke? Now? Well my nephew just arrived, but maybe I can stop by for a bit right away before we settle down to dinner. See you in a few."

Phillips smiled at his aunt. "Sorry, Tom, I've just got to go this karaoke rehearsal at one of my girlfriend's. I won't be long." She kissed him on the cheek as she walked passed to the door. "See you two boys later."

Matt rolled his eyes and belched.

"Why don't we sit in the back yard and have a beer, Tom? I'm making some burgers, and we can sit out there and chat."

"Gosh, I'd love to, Uncle Matt."

As he walked out the back door, Phillips came into a yard that made him stop and look. A huge green expanse lay before him, surrounded on three sides by an 8-foot-high redwood fence. Half a dozen trees provided pleasant shade from the summer sun, and in one corner was a large fishpond. Matt walked over to a cement double barbecue where some coals were smoldering. "Nice, huh?" he said as Phillips took it in.

"You sure have it made."

"Here, Tom." Matt handed him a cold beer from a tub filled with bottles and chunks of ice. Matt popped one open and handed him a dish. "Remember these?"

"Sure do."

"I remembered potato sticks were your favorite when we visited so I thought I'd have some here for you for old times sake."

Phillips smiled at the thought of one of his comfort foods growing up, especially on cold, snowy winter nights in front of the TV with Mom, Dad and Kate.

By the time Matt had finished frying one batch of burgers and put on another, he had polished off half a dozen bottles of beer. Phillips looked at him funny.

"You're lookin' at me kinda shhtrange, there, m'boy. Anything on your old mind?"

"No, not really, Uncle Matt." But Phillips was uneasy.

"You're probly wondering why I drink so much."

"I'm just glad you're not driving anywhere." Matt didn't laugh at Phillips' half-hearted attempt at humor.

"You see all thish, thish house, thish yard. It's all bullshit."

Phillips wanted to speak but didn't.

"All thish shows appearances aren't worth a crap."

Matt opened another beer.

"Uncle Matt, what's the matter?"

His uncle stood and looked off over the tops of the trees on the edge of his yard, then turned to face Phillips. "You know who I envy?"

"Who is that, Uncle Matt?" Phillips answered.

"Last year your Aunt Millie and I went to Mexico, to Puerto Vallarta. One late afternoon as we sat on some chairs at the beach drinking a few beers, I saw these kids with nets, catching fish for supper or to sell to restaurants or some damn thing.

"It's them I envy, Tom. Those kids had no cares, no worry about what tomorrow might bring." The two men drank their beer and smelled the cooking burgers. "You know what, Uncle Matt?"

"What?"

"I'll bet those kids saw you and Aunt Millie sitting on those nice chairs, drinking that nice cold beer, and they envied you."

Matt snorted and chuckled scornfully.

"Bullshit."

Matt hung his head. Phillips was afraid his uncle was going to start crying right there in front of him.

"Uncle Matt?"

"My kids, Howard and Leslie. You remember them maybe? They hate me, Tom," he said, looking up.

"Why do you say that? I thought they were coming over tonight."

"They are, but to see you. They hardly ever talk to me."

"I think you're being harsh on yourself, Uncle …"

"Harsh, my ass. Tom, they want nothing to do with me. And do you know whose fault it is? My own. When they were growing up I was too busy with my work or my golf or all the other excuses I found for not being a father. I figured my duty stopped when I balled their mother, and now I'm paying the price for being a self-centered asshole.

"My failure with them is my biggest regret. You see this house, all we have here, the trappings of a contrived happiness? I'd give them all up if I could just make things right with them."

Phillips didn't know what to say.

"And…and, if that weren't enough…"

"What is it, Uncle Matt?"

"I'm sorry to lay all this shit on you, Tom, but it's been inside for me so long I just have to tell someone."

Phillips wondered how Matt could have been a resident of Akron for decades, lived in this house for maybe 20 years and not have a neighbor, friend or colleague he could talk to about what was aching inside his heart.

"Uncle Matt, talk to me all you want. I am ready to listen if you need."

Matt sat across from Tom at the picnic table, covered his mouth with the palm of his right hand and stared blankly at the ground.

"Tom…"

"Just a second, Uncle Matt. Let me check on the hamburgers." Phillips walked over to the barbecue. He picked one up with the spatula. "Looks done to me," he said. "I'll put them in the pan, okay?"

"Go for it, young man," Matt said. He handed Phillips a bottle of beer. "I already have one," he said and turned back to the barbecue.

"No, it's not for you. Pour it over the hamburgers in the pan, put on the cover and let them simmer for a bit."

"Is that why they taste so great?"

"I guess my secret's out, Tom."

Phillips did as he was told, returned to the picnic bench and sat across from his uncle. He looked at him and said, "You were saying?"

"Just a sec." Matt got up, went back into the house and into the bathroom off the master bedroom. He took a leak, splashed some water on his face and looked into the mirror. "Get a grip on yourself, man. He's more in control of himself than you are, and you're old enough to be his father."

Matt went into the kitchen, poured two cups of coffee and went back outside. Tom was still sitting on the bench, his head turned upward, his eyes closed, grabbing some of the late sunshine. "Here," his uncle said and put a cup of coffee in front of him. "Now where were?"

"Oh, yes." Matt hesitated and took a breath. "You know, Tom, what I tell you has to be just between us. I've not confided this to anyone else, but I'm so pent up inside I just have to talk. And you seem to be a good enough sort, at least your mom and dad always talk well of you."

"I like to think I'm a good listener. Now what's up?"

"It's Millie. She's on this kick where she has to always look and act young, like this karaoke shit. But that's only the half of it. For the past year she's been going to these mate-swapping parties where she always manages to get bedded by someone about half her age.

"She tells me the next day it makes her feel young again. We always had a good sex life, but now that I'm an old fart I'm not good enough."

Phillips listened.

"Sometimes it's almost comical. One night she went upstairs with some young buck who looked like he was about 20 years old, and she was wearing that silly-ass watch you saw on her today. I figured if she gave the son of a bitch a hand job wearing that thing she would break her wrist.

"Just thinking of it while I stayed downstairs waiting for her made me laugh so hard I damn near pissed my pants."

"Can I ask you something?" Phillips interjected.

"Of course."

"Do you ever, uh, partake at these parties? Maybe if you did, it wouldn't bother you about Aunt Millie and you might even like it."

His uncle stared at him. "In the first place, most of the women at these things are young enough to be my Leslie. And in the second place, I could never. It would feel to me like I was cheating. Millie can deal with this, but I couldn't."

"So what do you do while you're waiting?"

"I generally sit in the living room and watch a baseball or football game and drink a few beers. Then when Millie is finished, we go out for a late snack and back home.

"I remember one time this young thing in a short skirt sat down at the other end of the couch where I was. She flirted with me and kept moving her hand up her thigh. Finally she looked right at me and said, 'Want some?'"

"And?"

"I looked right back and said, 'Are you kidding? The Dodgers-Reds game is on ESPN!'"

Phillips laughed so hard this time it was almost he who pissed his pants. He bent over, clapped his uncle on the shoulder and said, "Uncle Matt, you are too much. You and Millie are too much. You're not putting me on about this, are you?"

He raised his right arm. "Swear to God."

Before either could say anything more, a man and woman walked into the yard from the back door. "Hi, Dad," one of them called out.

"Hey, kids, thanks for coming over. Do you remember your cousin, Tom Phillips? He had hoped you would stop by and he could say hi. Tom, this is my son and daughter, Howard and Leslie."

Phillips shook Howard's hand and smiled at Leslie. They looked so evenly matched standing there and fit so well together they could have been a happily married couple if you didn't know they were brother and sister.

"I remember we met years and years ago," Howard said. "So how are you, Tom? What brings you to Akron?"

"I'm just passing through on my way back to visit my folks in Indiana. It sure is nice here. This is a beautiful home."

"Yes, I guess it is pretty nice," answered Leslie. "We don't come over that much, but when we do we always enjoy it."

The back door opened again. "How are my two lovely children?" Millie sang out as she walked up to her two kids and put an arm around each. "Tom, aren't they precious?"

"Mom, for heaven's sake, you make us sound like we're your puppies," Howard said and squirmed away from his mother's grasp.

"Well, you're my babies, and that's good enough for me to fawn all over you."

Matt came over. "Food's on. Come and get it."

The five of them crowded over to a table laden with food. Beer-soaked burgers, crisp hard rolls, potato salad, fruit salad, corn on the cob, pie, potato chips, cheese, crackers and big, fat, sour dill pickles. Phillips stood back and looked with a grin at a feast that everyone took for granted as just another day at the table. Were they better off than the boys fishing off the coast of Mexico? Are a full belly and tormented soul better than poverty with peace of mind? Who knows? Just pass the potato salad.

As night fell on the family and friend, squirrels danced along the outer edge of the lawn, perhaps toward a hiding place nestled under a tree. Phillips yawned and decided it was time to hit the sack. He had another drive tomorrow, off to see Kate in Toledo. "G'night everybody," he said and retreated to the house.

"G'night, Tom," the four answered in unison.

"Tom, it was good seeing you again," Howard called. "Same here," echoed Leslie.

"Tom, be sure to have some breakfast with us before you leave," Matt added. Millie edged over to her husband and took his hand. "We're so happy you could stop in for a visit," she said as he opened the door, walked inside and went up to the guestroom.

Phillips stripped to his shorts, took out his notebook to write about the day in his diary, then closed it and sat on the edge of the bed. There was nothing he wanted to write down. He went to the window, pulled aside the curtain and looked up at the clear, starry sky. Down below, Matt, Millie, Howard and Leslie were laughing and talking, a family sharing the waning hours of a summer day. From all appearances this was a perfectly functional family enjoying each other's company. His mind went to work:

Gosh, Matt seems happy now, Millie seems happy, the kids seem happy. Is all this just in Matt's mind? Is he just bullshitting me about those swapping parties she drags him off to? I wish I could get Millie's side of this, but you don't exactly come up to your aunt and say, so do you really like getting boned by a stranger while your husband sits downstairs watching ESPN? And even if this is true, who is to say what is functional and what isn't? Are the problems of this family any worse or better than those of another? Is Matt the one who loves? Millie? The kids? All of them? None of them? And am I in any position to judge these people? I'm the one who's planning to blow his brains out in the bedroom I grew up in because I am afraid to face the future knowing I will be diseased and deteriorating.

Maybe what really matters is that these people are getting along now, at this moment. They shouldn't ask for any more than that. I guess I shouldn't either. And yet I do.

Phillips turned away and got into bed. Just before falling asleep he had one last thought. Hey, Uncle Matt doesn't eat like a pig anymore.

In the yard below, the family talked into the night.

CHAPTER 17

▼

FAMILY

Peggy was in the kitchen, up early as always. Age had slowed Phillips' mother, but it hadn't stopped her. "I've got too much to do. I can't get old, and I can't stop," she would say to Joe when he told her to take it easier on herself. And besides, she loved the early-morning hours when the world was still asleep. She liked to think she had a corner of it to herself, and indeed she had.

The sun was peeking through the kitchen windows. Peggy had always loved looking out that window most of all, whether it was crusted with snow and ice in the winter or whether, like now, she could see the old apple tree in the yard readying its produce for another autumn. She still hadn't shaken the nagging feeling something was wrong, but that was not important. What truly mattered was that her little sandman would be home in a few days.

Peggy hummed as she prepared her breakfast, sipped a cup of tea and thought of how she couldn't wait to see Joe later in the morning. He would be waiting as always, missing her until she walked through the door to his room at the nursing home.

In Washington, Helena and Bea went about their workday routines, each separately apprehensive about the trip to Indiana later in the week. They had decided to travel together and take a suite at a South Bend hotel. They might be acquaintances, and for the task ahead maybe even companions, but that wouldn't extend to them sharing a bed together. Even friendship has its limits.

Phillips arose at 7 in Akron. He wanted to leave his aunt and uncle's house without any more conversation or uncomfortable revelations. He was ready for the visit to Kate, someone he could count on to be centered or well grounded or whatever the catch phrase was these days for someone who had their shit together.

Sure enough, everyone was still asleep as he walked quietly from the bedroom. By the looks of things, with four pairs of grass-covered shoes neatly put in one corner of the kitchen, even Howard and Leslie had stayed the night. Families! If they didn't fight about things or have issues, there'd be nothing to keep them together.

Phillips tore a piece of paper from his notebook and scribbled on it:

> Dear Aunt Millie and Uncle Matt:
>
> It was nice seeing you again, and Howard and Leslie too. Thanks for your hospitality. And Uncle Matt, don't worry, I won't share your secret of what makes a great hamburger!
>
> Love,
> Tom

He attached the note to the refrigerator with one of those $2.99 magnets from Disneyland he found stuck on the door and tiptoed out of the house.

It was misting as Phillips started his car. He smiled at the memory of those rainy summer days when he was growing up, and today had all the promise of being one. The skies were leaden. The grass and flowers smelled fresh. He drove to at a fast-food restaurant for some hash browns, a couple of egg sandwiches and coffee, then hit the highway.

Phillips was right. Two hours of open road were between Akron and Toledo, and it rained all the way to his sister's front step.

Kate bounded up at the first ring of the door bell.

"Tom!" She hugged him close and kissed him on the cheek. Phillips returned the affection. "Gosh, how I've missed you. Come in, please. Let me get a towel for you to dry yourself."

Phillips had gotten soaked on the walk up to Kate's house, a two-bedroom cottage with a small garden in the back. She could have afforded to buy something much bigger in a more upscale part of town. Like Tom she had learned to live frugally but well. And besides, this place suited her needs just fine. She was content and happy. As Phillips surmised, she had her shit together.

"Kate, I've missed you too. Listen to us. You'd think we hadn't seen each other in years when it's been less than six months."

"Sometimes it feels like years, doesn't it?"

"That it does."

"Can I get you something?"

"No, I'm fine, thanks. Hey, don't you have to work today?"

"I'm going in later this morning. Then I thought we could go somewhere tonight. There's someone I want you to meet."

Phillips and Kate held hands and walked to the couch. "Wow, you've met someone? Maybe I will take a cup of coffee so we can talk for a bit before you go to work."

"Coming right up."

Phillips looked around the living room. He always felt comfortable here, probably because Kate's place reminded him so much of his own. Her furnishings were tasteful and comfortable, not ostentatious. He walked over and picked up the picture of his parents taken on their 40th wedding anniversary. As he put it down, he noticed another one on the mantle that had not been there before – of a buoyant Kate standing on the deck of a motor boat next to an equally buoyant, rugged-looking, tanned, presumed-to-be boyfriend.

Kate came back into the living room carrying a tray with two cups of coffee and four pieces of buttered rye toast. "Your favorite, Tom. See? A sister never forgets."

As she put the tray down on the coffee table, she noticed Phillips looking at the picture. "Oh, I see you've noticed the man in my life."

"This is the man you've met?"

"Sure. You sound surprised."

Phillips sat next to Kate on the couch, took a sip of coffee and a bite of toast. "Ah, perfect as always."

"Thanks. Now, what you were saying?"

"Oh, I don't know. This guy just doesn't look like the type I had imagined you finding."

"And what type was that?"

"I suppose I figured you'd meet a more buttoned-down person, a businessman or college professor, something like that."

"What makes you think he isn't? And really, Tom, I'd always figured you more for the professor type."

"Me? Why?"

"You just seem more of a learned guy, someone involved in the world of books and writing and thinking."

Phillips had never really thought about it. Maybe she had a point. Too late now anyway. "What does your friend do for a living? And I presume he has a name."

"Of course, smarty-pants. His name is Matt Edwards." She added with a smile, "And he's an auto mechanic."

"Hmm. Well, hey, Dad worked with his hands all his life, and there isn't a better man around, so who am I to judge?"

"Thank you, Tom." Kate leaned over and kissed Phillips on the forehead.

"Tell me about your Matt Edwards."

"He's 45, a real outdoors type as you could probably guess. Married twice, two kids, both in their 20s and on their own. And before you ask, yes, he does have issues but we're working on them."

"He sounds like a real project to me, Kate."

"Isn't every man?"

"Some more than others, I suppose. But I'm sure you know what you're doing. I am happy you found someone, and I will tell you you are one of the few people I know who handles relationships well."

Kate laughed, knowing it wasn't difficult since most of her relationships had lasted about an hour. "How do you mean?"

"Most people I know bitch about their partner, and then when they're free, they bitch about being alone. You seem to handle both well."

"Well, I thank you for the compliment. And yes, I do try. Matt and I believe in each other and the person each of us is. He envies me for coming from such a stable family, and I make allowances for his growing up in a broken home with contentious parents. That explains a lot."

Phillips bristled. "Don't tell me you've become one of those who will explain away misbehavior by an adult because of their upbringing. Tell me you haven't gone that route, Kate."

His sister looked lovingly at the photograph, then went over and ran the tip of her index finger along the picture of Matt. "Let's just say I'm not as adamant against that as I once was. Anyway, you'll get to meet him tonight and see for yourself what a good guy he is."

"Done. I hereby declare a truce. At least he'll keep your engine running."

"That's not the only engine he keeps running."

"Kate?"

"Big brother, now we're even for when you used to tease me about Mom and Dad screwing."

Phillips got up. "I think it's time I took a nap and took my things in."

"Good idea. I've got to get into work anyway. Make yourself at home, I'll be back about 5. We'll be going to a bar and grill downtown tonight for dinner, but it's very casual. See you then."

Kate kissed Phillips on the cheek, and he kissed her back.

He awoke from his nap at 2:30 and went into the backyard. The rain had stopped, but the angry sky lingered. The overcast, cool afternoon suited him wonderfully.

Phillips looked around. The yard was meticulous, no weeds, all corners neatly squared off. The small garden had green peppers and Roma tomatoes, both family favorites. A weeping willow hung majestically in a corner of the yard. Phillips found a lounge chair, dried it with a towel he found in the garage and sat.

He pulled out the cell phone, punched in Natalie's number and left a message on her voicemail that he would arrive in Chicago sometime Wednesday afternoon. Mom was next.

"Hello?" Phillips loved the sweetness of his mother's voice. It had been there whenever he needed it all of his life. "Hi, Mom, I'm at Kate's."

"Tommy! I'm glad you made it to your sister's. When will you be home?"

"Probably Friday."

"You just be careful and get here when you can."

"I will, Mom. Bye and see you soon. I love you."

"I love you, Tommy."

Natalie and Mom were the two most important women in his life, always had been, and always would be. Content after his calls, Phillips laid back on the lounge, lost his thoughts in the swirling gray clouds and closed his eyes.

He saw the gun go off. His eyes closed, his body slumped and then he fell down, down, spiraling into a fiery abyss. His body tried to speak but couldn't, tried to move but couldn't, tried to right itself and run, run as fast as it could, but couldn't. Finally his body was able to scream. "No!" Then louder, "No! No!"

"Tom. Tommy. Wake up!" Phillips saw Kate. Was he dead? Was he dreaming? "Where am I?" he asked.

"Tom, you're here, in my backyard. You were sleeping when I got home and then I heard you screaming. Are you alright?"

"I, I think so." He sat up. The sun was peeking through the clouds.

"What time is it?"

"5:15. Still want to go out tonight?"

"Sure, just let me get myself straightened out."

He walked around the yard, smelling the flowery fragrances set off by the rain, then went inside, took a shower and called to Kate that he'd be ready to leave at 7:30.

Matt was waiting when they entered the bar and grill.

He was strong, not big, but with a powerful build. His chest, arms and shoulders were those of someone used to physical work and his handshake firm and unmistaken. His eyes were gentle, and Phillips took an immediate liking to this man who loved his sister.

"Tom, I've heard a lot about you," Matt said as he pulled out a chair for Kate and the three of them sat. "Kate here certainly cares for her brother."

"Matt, I'm happy to meet you. As long as you take good care of her I won't have to get tough with you." Phillips smiled as he said it, and the three of them laughed. They engaged in small talk, about life in Ohio and Washington, about their interests and their parents and kids. Phillips bragged about Natalie whenever he could, but Matt was reserved about his two children.

"I don't see my son and daughter much. Their mother and I had a pretty brutal divorce and I'm afraid I let my hostility to her interfere with my love and caring for the kids."

"I'll bet if you told them you loved them and why you pulled away they would understand," Phillips said. "Saying I'm sorry can do wonders."

Matt smiled ruefully. "There's a lot of that going around."

"A lot of what going around?" Phillips asked.

"Apologizing," Matt answered. "Saying I'm sorry, the great eraser in modern society. I'm sorry I got drunk and killed your wife. I'm sorry I treated you like shit at work. I'm sorry I ignored you kids by taking out my problems with your mother on you.

"Saying sorry doesn't mean shit."

Kate put her right arm around Matt's shoulders, covered his left hand with hers and kissed him. "Honey, we'll make it right. We can work it out. I love you." Matt smiled at her and kissed her back. Funny how men have the reputation of being the stronger of the species when it's the women all along.

The three fell silent. Finally Kate smiled and said, "I'm sure all of us do things we regret. It's part of becoming and being adults. C'mon, lighten up."

She lifted her glass of wine. "Here's to lightening up."

"Hear! Hear!" Matt and Phillips said in unison. Both laughed, and then Kate laughed too.

They ordered dinner, the subject turned light again and so did their mood. Kate looked across the room and waved to a woman getting a drink at the bar. She motioned her over.

Kate got up as the woman approached the table. "Maria! Gosh, it's great seeing you here. How've you been?"

"Just fine, Kate, how about you?"

"Doing wonderfully, especially tonight. You've met my friend Matt, haven't you?"

"I have," Maria said, extended her hand to him and then turned to look at Phillips. "And who's this? Let me guess, your brother Tom."

"Right you are, Maria. Tom, this is my friend, Maria Navoli."

She extended her hand to Phillips, who shook it gently. "Nice to meet you, Maria."

"And you, Tom. Just passing through?"

"Yes, I'm on my way to Indiana."

"Kate, why don't you, Matt and your brother stop over at our table after dinner if you have time and we can chat?" Maria asked. She looked at Kate, then at Tom as she said it.

"We'd love to," Kate said. "That OK with you fellas?"

"Fine by me," Matt answered.

"Likewise," Phillips said.

"See you in a bit, Maria," Kate said as her friend returned to her table. "I met Maria here about a year ago. Great lady," Kate said. "She's a professor, seems happy with her life and her work."

"You seem to be too, Kate, aren't you?" Phillips asked.

"I am, sure, though work can be a grind. Everybody is meeting happy these days. Meetings to schedule other meetings, to talk about meetings we just had, to talk about meetings we're going to have. I swear if the Revolutionary Army had dicked around like this we'd still be a colony."

They had a good laugh, paid their dinner bill, then walked to Maria's table. "Hey, glad you could join us," she said. "Stella and Sandy," she said, gesturing to the two other women at the table, "meet Kate, Matt and Tom."

They brought over extra chairs, ordered drinks and sat down to talk. Phillips ended up sitting next to Maria.

"How long are you in town, Tom?" she asked.

"Just until tomorrow. Do you live here?"

"No. I'm from Lafayette. I'm visiting some friends but am mostly on my way up to see some ballgames. I'm headed to Chicago to see the Cubs and White Sox, then to Milwaukee to see the Brewers at County Stadium before they tear it down after this season."

"You must really like baseball."

"I sure do."

"Are your friends going along?"

"No, I'm going myself. I'm a big girl, Tom."

Phillips studied her, then said, "That you are. Kate tells me you're a professor?"

"Yes, I teach political science at Purdue."

"That must be interesting."

"It is. I went to work as a stewardess right out of college, got the wild streak out of me, came back for my master's and Ph.D. and settled into the academic life in Lafayette. Although I still do love traveling, I really enjoy working with the students, and in the summers I can set my own pace, like going to baseball games when I want. I work part-time as a waitress at a local coffee shop just for a change, and I can visit my parents for a couple of weeks back home in D.C."

"Your parents live in Washington?"

"They do. Kate tells me you live there?"

"For some years now. I love it."

"I do too, or at least visiting. Say, how about giving me your business card? The next time I visit maybe I can call you and we have lunch or something."

"Sure," Phillips said. He wanted to mean it but wasn't sure if he should.

Kate walked over, smiled at Phillips and Maria and leaned over and kissed him on the cheek. "I've got to go, big brother. You look like you're having fun here, so why not stay a while longer and catch a cab or something?"

"Let me walk you to your car."

Phillips turned to Maria. "I'll be back," he said.

"I'll be here," Maria answered. She smiled.

Kate kissed Matt good night, then walked arm in arm with Phillips. They stopped at her car. "Looks like you and Maria have really hit it off," she said. "The two of you were sitting there talking like there's no one else in the room."

Phillips looked over, surprised. Kate was right. They leaned their backs against her car and talked.

"Oh, we just are chatting about nothing in particular."

"Let me tell you, she'd be a fine catch. She's dated a whole bunch of Mister Wrongs and is really looking for one special man. Like yourself."

"Kate, Kate, I think you're jumping the gun a bit aren't you? And besides, isn't she a lot younger than me?"

"She's 36. What are you, 48? Only 12 years. That's nothing. Listen to me. She's wonderful. Loves to travel, loves sports, loves to cook, a really wonderful person. And totally available."

"Ach, I don't know, Kate."

"You're not afraid of her, are you?"

"Afraid?"

"Yes, afraid. Lots of men are afraid of independent women, especially attractive independent women. That's why so many attractive independent women are alone when they wouldn't be if more men had the balls to love them. And that's why I love Matt."

Phillips looked over at his sister. "Why is that?"

"Because he isn't afraid to love me."

Phillips opened the door to Kate's car and closed it behind her after she got behind the wheel and started the engine. "See you later," Phillips said. "I'll be quiet."

"Remember what I said. She has a big heart, Tom, and people like her come around once in a lifetime."

As Phillips started back, he looked at his watch and realized he'd been gone over half an hour. "She's probably gone by now," he said, but still picked up his pace just a bit. He was struck by how much Maria seemed like Helena, had the same physique, the same beautiful blue eyes, the same sense of self and independence. He'd often marveled at how gracefully Helena went through life, seeming at ease whether she was at a beach party, a bar or a formal dinner. Was Maria like that too?

When Phillips returned to the bar, the crowd had thinned. Maria remained, alone, at her table.

"I wasn't sure you would be coming back, but I hung around just in case," she said.

"I said I would."

They ordered cappuccino and talked into the evening about traveling, D.C., politics, Indiana, baseball and each other until closing time. "Guess it's time to go," Phillips said.

"I guess it is. May I drive you back to Kate's place? I've been there so I know just where it is."

"Sure."

Maria drove slowly, wanting to talk more to this man Tom Phillips. She was not one to rush to judgment, nor did she easily fall for a man. If anything, her friends told her, she was too reticent, too cautious, too unwilling to take a chance. And yet she admitted to herself as she drove the two of them through the quiet streets of Toledo that she had enjoyed Phillips' company and perhaps would like to get to know him better. When she finally pulled up to the front of Kate's house, she looked into his eyes. "I've sure enjoyed meeting you, Tom. You're just like your sister said you were."

"I've enjoyed meeting you as well, Maria. Thanks for the ride and the good conversation."

He got out of the car and walked up the sidewalk to Kate's front door. Maria opened the passenger's side window and called out to him. "I'll call you next month when I'm in Washington."

"Please do. Good night. And thanks for the lift." He opened the door and waved. She waved back and headed to her motel, feeling very much alone in the night.

Phillips walked quietly into Kate's house, got a soda from the fridge, then went to the guestroom. He took out his diary.

Tuesday, July 11

It feels like it's been a while since I opened this. It feels good to write, especially after an eventful couple of days, from the total craziness of Uncle Matt and Aunt Millie's family to Kate's strength and surprise boyfriend. I sure hope his first name shared with my poor uncle in Akron is nothing more than coincidence!

Phillips felt the sudden urge to go to the gun in his duffel bag. He took it out, turned it over, sneered at the uncaring piece of metal that in four days would end what had taken 48 years to build. He put it back and returned to his diary.

> *Is this really the answer? Nobody around me has their shit together any more or less than I do. But I don't see any signs that any of them intend to end it all. Then again, they don't see any signs I plan to do it either. I expect they'll all be pretty surprised when they find me dead Saturday. Don't you hear all the time about people killing themselves who seemed happy and carefree and together, yet it turns out there was something inside gnawing and overpowering?*
> *I've thought about maybe delaying this, maybe there is something to getting good medical help, and maybe my family will support me. But what if I'm wrong, what if these hopes turn out to be nothing more than empty wishes. Mom and Dad won't be around forever, Kate will have her own family, Helena already does, and Bea might go too. The timing of this just looks so right. Saturday is the time to do it, so do it I will.*
> *I wonder what Maria is doing now.*

Phillips put away his diary and opened his Bible, took a sip of Coke, put the book on his lap and fell asleep.

C H A P T E R 1 8

▼

CHICAGO

The travel alarm clock read 6 a.m. Phillips awoke, his Bible underneath him, the light beside the bed still on. Taped to the mirror was a note:

Tom, I went in to work early since I'll be back with you early next week and I have to work ahead. Can't wait to spend more time with you in Indiana. I love you, Kate.

Phillips sat up to read the note, then slumped back on the bed. In all likelihood, he would never see his sister again since she probably would be coming in late Friday and he would end it all Saturday morning. "This is madness," he said to himself and looked up at the ceiling, a knot forming in his stomach.

He had hoped to sleep in after the late night Tuesday, but there was no way that could happen now. After laying there awhile, Phillips dressed quickly, made the bed, packed and left.

He left no note for his sister.

The drive to Chicago normally took Phillips four hours, but today he made it in three. He wanted to get away from Toledo, from Kate, from the horrid realization of what he was going to do to himself. He tried the radio, found an oldies station and before long was singing along with his favorites by the Temptations, Four Tops, Martha and the Vandellas and one he really loved, *It's Gonna Take a Miracle.*

The music brought him back to his high school years. He smiled at the memory of the clinch and makeout music when a guy was happy if the songs put his date in the mood for some tongue, and if he was really lucky got to second base with her. He chuckled when he remembered how Natalie asked him what clinch music was. "Oh, you mean slow jammin'," she answered. This was progress? A clinch dance was slow jammin', banging was bumping uglies and getting tongue was now passe for kids who now started screwing in elementary school. He was glad Natalie had made it unscathed through those years. Hadn't she?

The knot in his stomach was almost gone when he turned his key to Natalie's apartment. It was cool his daughter trusted and loved her Dad enough to let him come and go at her place. "Your latch-key father," is how he often jokingly referred to himself when making arrangements to be in Chicago.

"God, how I love it here," he said as he entered her place on Fargo Avenue on the Far North side of Chicago. His daughter lived in an old neighborhood, on the second story of a brownstone that had the charm and ambiance of the big city and one huge perk: cable TV, meaning he could watch the Cubs whenever he visited during the baseball season.

After letting himself in, Phillips laid down for a nap, arose two hours later, made himself two pastrami sandwiches with a whole dill pickle on the side, cracked open a beer and turned on the TV. It was almost game time and he felt better.

Before settling in, he went over to the closet. Natalie always kept a few of his things on hand for when he visited, and one of them was a Cubs cap. As Phillips took it off the hook he noticed the Made in Bangladesh label. He frowned. "Some poor bastard works for pennies a day to make these throwaway caps, and here I am whimpering about some disease that won't get me for years while I have never wanted for a single thing in 48 years."

Phillips looked off, put on the cap and muttered "Fuck Bangladesh." As he sat in front of the TV, he wondered if Maria was there.

In the grandstand along the first-base line, Maria had a beer and a hot dog piled high with onions and relish. She wondered if Phillips was watching the game.

The day was clear and beautiful in Indiana. Peggy picked up the phone on the second ring. It was Kate.

"Hi, Mom. I was wondering if you need me to help you with anything for Saturday. I was planning to come in late Friday but can make it earlier if you want."

"No, honey, everything is taken care of. You stick to your plans. Bea and Helena called and said they can join us too." Peggy paused, then spoke again. "Kate, when Tom visited with you, did he seem alright?"

"Sure, Mom, same old Tom. Why do you ask?"

"Oh, I don't know. I just have this feeling something is wrong. It's probably just me."

"In fact, Tom met a friend of mine and it seemed they hit it off real well. She's a great person and I am sure would make a great partner for the right person."

"Tom needs someone."

"He does, Mom. Hey, I've got to run. Since I'll be coming there so late I can just let myself in. So I'll see you then if you're still up, or Saturday morning. I love you. This weekend will be just great."

"Bye, Kate. It will. I love you. See you soon."

Peggy still wasn't convinced as she hung up the phone. Something was nagging at her, and while sitting on the swing in the back yard she decided to talk to Joe about it. That day on her visit to the nursing home, she poured out her fears to her beloved husband. As she left the room to return home, she stopped and looked back. "Talk to your son, Joe."

Phillips walked over to the TV and shut it off. The Cubs were losing. Again. "What else is new," he said, went to the fridge and got another beer, then opened his wallet, fished out Father Luke's business card and called the number.

"Hello," answered a female voice.

"Hello," answered Phillips. "I'm Tom Phillips, a friend of Father Jonathan Luke's from Washington. He said he would be at this number visiting in Chicago."

"He is here, yes. I am his sister, Dorothy. Let me go get him for you."

Father Luke came shortly to the phone. "Thomas, I am glad you called. Have you had a good trip?"

"Very nice, Father Luke. And you?"

"Wonderful as always. It's a delight whenever I can get back to the Midwest and to spend some time with my sister."

"Father, I was hoping we could get together tomorrow to chat. Do you have time?"

"Of course. There is a wonderful hot dog stand on the lakefront, and the weather is so beautiful now. How about if we meet in front of the Shedd Aquarium in Grant Park at 1, grab a couple of Chicago hot dogs from that stand and sit on a bench along the lake? Most conducive to baring one's soul, or finding it."

"Sounds like a plan, Father. See you there at 1 tomorrow."

"Till then, Thomas. Peace be with you."

As Phillips hung up, the front door opened and Natalie walked in. She ran to her father and hugged him. "Daddy, I was hoping you'd be here." She kissed him on the neck. "Are you ready for Saturday?" she asked.

Phillips looked into her eyes, stunned. "What do you mean?" he blurted.

"The party, Daddy, the party. What did you think I meant?"

"Oh, I forgot all about it. Yeah, yeah, I'm all set for it. Say, sweetie, what are our plans tonight?"

Natalie looked at him. "You're sure you're alright. We can stay in if you like."

"No, I want to go out. Let's have some fun."

"Let's go for it. Wanna leave now?"

"Sure."

"Got a boyfriend yet?"

"Nah. Many are called but few are chosen, Daddy."

Phillips laughed a deep laugh that rose from his belly. It felt good to be with his daughter again. "So where are we going?"

"How about drinks on Rush Street, then dinner at a ribs house nearby?"

"Sounds delightful." Phillips couldn't get over, probably never would, how quickly his daughter had grown. It seemed like only yesterday they were at Disneyland, she wearing some silly Mickey Mouse ears and begging for cotton candy. Now here she was, a grown woman, making their plans for the evening. It made him happy and also a little bit sad, perhaps the lot of all parents everywhere.

Rush Street was jammed with the happy hour crowd, and after a couple of beers, Phillips and Natalie found themselves wearing bibs and sharing a huge plate of ribs, accompanied by mounds of mashed potatoes, corn on the cob and cole slaw. Someone else in the room was interested in sharing as well. Phillips and their waitress had made eye contact as soon as she brought over the menu, and their flirtation continued through the meal. She was a beefy blonde wanna-be with a Jesus Christ tattoo on her right bicep. Phillips loved two-tones, blonde hair (even if dyed) on top and black between the legs.

As he went to pay the bill, Phillips noticed she had written on the back, Hi, I'm Nicole. Call me at home after 11, with the phone number double-underlined. With that, he and Natalie caught a cab back to her apartment.

It had been a long day. Phillips sat up in bed absently reading the Bible, talking himself out of calling the waitress. He turned off the light, tossed and turned, then finally sat up and pronounced, "If I can't get interested in pussy anymore, I might as well be dead."

Even he had to smile at that, turned on the light, got out the receipt from his wallet and called the number.

"Hello, Nicole, this is Tom Phillips from the restaurant."

"Tom, what a nice name. I wasn't sure you'd call."

"Neither was I."

"But you're calling now."

"That I am. Wanna do something?"

"Sure, how about catching a cab and coming to my place?"

"How do you know I'm not some kind of nut?"

"I'll take my chances."

Phillips laughed. "Can I bring anything?"

"Tom, I have a case of Old Style, a hot pepperoni pizza and a box of French ticklers. I think we're all set."

Phillips was at her front door in 30 minutes. Nicole was waiting for him.

He confirmed she was a two-tone on her living room floor, and after they had some pizza he went down on her again as she sat on the sofa. Pinching her nipples gave her a nice orgasm. Neither Phillips nor Nicole got much sleep that night.

The next morning, after treating his one-night friend to a breakfast of eggs Benedict, pumpernickel toast, hash browns, V8 and tea, he returned to Natalie's apartment just as she was getting ready for work.

"Got lucky, eh, Daddy?" she said with a twinkle in her eye.

"What do you know about getting lucky, young lady?"

"Daddy, I'm 24 for heaven's sake."

"Uh huh. What are your plans for today? I may stay another day or may head back tonight. That okay if I stick around until tomorrow?"

"Of course. But I have to work late today so if you leave tonight I may not see you before. So I guess I'd catch up with you Saturday."

Phillips had tears in his eyes as he hugged his daughter goodbye, leaving Natalie puzzled as she walked down the stairs to the street. "Why would he react like that when I'm going to see him in just a few days?" she wondered. The thought stayed with her as she boarded the subway for work.

Phillips saw Father Luke waiting when he walked up to the aquarium. They shook hands warmly. "Good to see you again, Father," Phillips said.

"And it is good to see you, Thomas. Come, there is a hot dog stand nearby in the park that is out of this world."

Phillips was amused as he and Father Luke walked, intrigued by the priest's enthusiasm over the Chicago hot dogs that awaited them. They bounded up to the stand. Each ordered two Vienna sausages on soft buns, Phillips' piled with dehydrated onions, relish, sauerkraut and spicy mustard, Father Luke's with pickles and peppers. Both added a large order of fries and a 20-ounce bottle of Coke.

Carrying their booty, the two men found a bench overlooking Lake Michigan. A few children played on the beach, lovers walked by holding hands, two old men sat under a tree listening to a baseball game, boats pulled water skiers in the distance. The sky was cloudless, the sun warm.

"Tell me, Thomas, do you like football?" Father Luke asked as he raised one of the glorious dogs to his mouth.

Phillips was mildly taken aback, expecting the priest to ask about his state of mind or health, not about sports like millions of other junkies across the land probably would have.

"As a matter of fact I do. I am hoping the Colts do well this year, though I am not sure they are Super Bowl caliber. And you?"

"Well, I am partial to the Ravens, and with their defense could be formidable."

Phillips chewed on a fry. "The Ravens? Sorry, Father, but even if this is the year 2000 and the dawn of a New Millennium, the gods can't smile that much on your team. Baltimore winning the Super Bowl? What a laugh."

"We shall see." Father Luke finished his meal, put his head back to get some sun on his face, then stretched his arm on the back of the bench and pierced Phillips with his intent gray eyes.

He got right to the point. "Tell me, Thomas, have you resolved the issues you spoke of during our meeting in Washington?"

"No, actually I still don't see any easy way out of my situation. I have tried dealing with my thoughts through a diary, been reading the Bible, even looked for that sign you spoke of. Nothing has worked."

Father Luke looked at Phillips, then gazed out at the horizon.

"Thomas, you don't find the sign, it finds you. It is simply up to you to recognize it."

"I don't see the difference."

"There is one, believe me. When I saw those children, I had no idea where life would take me. I just knew it would take me in a new direction. The Lord doesn't chart our journey, he points us toward it. It is up to us to make the walk. He is there if we stumble."

"You know, Father, I have seen people on this trip who give me hope, others who should make me feel lucky. And yet I feel nothing, only an emptiness inside, a sense of having no direction where once I felt I knew exactly where I wanted to be and to go.

"I am lost."

The priest gently touched Phillips' shoulder. "A pastor whom I am very fond of used to counsel troubled people, those who had lost all hope and resolve. He told them to think of their life's circumstances at that time as if they were walking in a forest, had been walking for what seemed like forever. There was no wildlife around, no sunlight, only trees, to the side, in front, in back, above. Keep walking, he told them, always keep walking and do not stop. Because you never know if just a few feet ahead of you the forest ends and in front of you opens a sunlit meadow of breathtaking beauty, waiting for you to lie down in the grass, make a home and find your heart."

"There is no meadow for me, Father. I'm scared."

"Thomas, Thomas." Father Luke reached into his pocket and took out a small, worn Bible. "Listen to these words from Psalm 40":

I waited patiently for the Lord, and he inclined unto me, and heard my cry.

He brought me up out of a horrible pit, set my feet upon a rock, and established my goings.

"Look and listen, my friend. The Lord is here for you. I am here for you. Many are here for you. Have faith, and if you do, you will not be afraid of what life has in store. Look for beauty and grace. They are all around you, in a bank of clouds, the peacefulness of a summer night, the laughter of children, the eyes of those who believe in God."

Phillips took a drink of Coke and closed his eyes. He spoke on a whim. "Father, what are you doing Saturday?"

"Well, I will be with my sister, then heading back to Washington on Sunday. Why?"

"My folks are having a get-together at their house in South Bend and I would really like you to meet them."

"I don't know ..."

"I will arrange for and pay for a rental car and give you directions. Please?"

About the last thing Father Luke wanted to do was end his visit to Chicago by going out of his way to spend time with people he didn't know. But as a man of God and a human being with a calling, that was precisely why he knew he must go. And so he agreed.

"I'll call you later today with the arrangements, Father," Phillips said as they stood and said goodbye. "And thank you again."

Phillips watched the priest leave the park, returned to the bench and looked out at the lake. "Now why did I do that?" he asked himself. "Someone to talk me out of this? Or the more the merrier when they find my body in the bedroom with a gunshot in my head?"

He was still sitting on the bench when day turned to dusk.

CHAPTER 19

▼

THE MAN IN THE MIRROR

Instead of calming him, the meeting with Father Luke had put Phillips in a depressed funk. An afternoon that started out well ended in a miserable evening. "He's got his shit together. Me, I'm headed to vegetable land." Phillips talked so loudly to himself that a couple of passersby stopped to look as he left the park and headed up Michigan Avenue.

Worse, Phillips couldn't remember where he was or how to get where he wanted to go. Whether it was his own railing against a perceived unfairness of life or him having another Big A moment he couldn't know. And it didn't matter. Traffic and people poured by as he slowly walked up the street trying to get his bearings.

"Look for the meadow, look for the meadow" kept going through his mind, though he didn't know why. He turned up a side street. There, amid the parking garages, office buildings and hustle of the evening in the big city, he saw a neon sign blinking, on and off, on and off, on and off.

Emma's Coffee Shop.

He went inside.

As he found a table near the window, Phillips looked around and noticed a mixture of diners. There were suits, leftover hippies, the down and out, a couple of teenagers. Something about the manner of the crowd intrigued him, as if they were not eating here so much as resting or getting a breath of fresh air. He began to get himself straight again, remembered his name, that he had come from the park where he had met with Father Luke, was off to his daughter's place, then headed to Indiana and his parents' house.

Phillips put his face in his hands and rubbed his eyes.

"Hi," came a female voice.

Phillips looked up. A smallish woman with bright red hair, light pink lipstick and a light-blue waitress's dress was looking at him. She smiled gently. "Can I get you anything, a glass of water perhaps?"

"Sure, that'd be nice." Phillips thought a second. "And how about a cup of coffee, a burger and fries?"

"Coming right up."

Phillips found a copy of the Chicago Tribune and read the sports pages as he waited for his food.

Presently the waitress brought his meal and smiled again. "You doing alright?"

"Sure. Don't I look alright?"

"You do now but not when you came in."

"You wouldn't be Emma by any chance, would you?" Phillips asked.

"One and the same."

"This is a cool place you have here."

"I'm glad you like it."

"Got a sec to sit with me?"

Emma slid into the seat across from him.

"So how did you get a place like this? I mean this feels almost like a way station rather than a restaurant."

"That's an interesting way of putting it, uh ..."

"Tom. Tom Phillips." He extended his hand, and Emma shook it.

"This place just kind of happened. My husband, his name was Edward, Eddie I called him, we had a husband-and-wife law practice. Very rewarding, very successful. Then Eddie was diagnosed with cancer and he died, just like that, six months later.

"He was a Vietnam vet, and though nobody proved it, we were both sure he got it from Agent Orange. On his deathbed, I promised that dear man I would let no one suffer if I could help. One day about two months later I was walking downtown, passed this very place, noticed it was for sale and bought it.

"That was eight years ago, and in that time I have become known as Emma who turns no one away if they are hungry and Emma who always listens if you have a care. Many of the people who come in, some of them right now as you and I sit here, just need a place to catch their breath before going on their way. Maybe a loved one is sick like my beloved Eddie was, or they are having marital problems, or their children are too much for them to handle at the moment. Whatever. I don't take away their burdens, but I like to think in my own small way I help them deal with whatever is hurting them at the moment.

"Tell me, Tom, how did you find me?"

"I saw the sign in the window."

"Ah."

Emma rose. "Well, Tom Phillips, whatever it is that brought you in here, I hope you can deal with it when you walk back outside." With that she smiled once again, shook his hand and walked toward the back of the restaurant, gently patting some customers on the back, picking up a dish here and there, exchanging a word with a young couple paying at the cash register. Phillips noticed the young man and woman hand over only a couple of coins with their bill. Both hugged Emma warmly before departing.

Emma walked back into the kitchen, smiling at the memory of her dead husband. "Eddie and Emma," she said to herself. "It sounded so right, it was so right."

"My husband, I honor you with my life."

The stop at Emma's had done Phillips a world of good. He finished his meal, caught a cab back to Natalie's and decided to speed up his itinerary by a day and return to South Bend that night. He had a lot to do.

First, he called to arrange a rental car, then called Father Luke to tell him the car would be delivered to his sister's place Saturday morning. He confirmed the address, gave him directions to his parents' house and surprised himself by saying "God bless you, Father" before hanging up.

Next, he called Mom, told her he would be there tonight but would arrive late and not to wait up for him.

Finally, he left a note for Natalie in an envelope on her pillow:

My sweet daughter –

You make me proud.

I love you,
Your Dad

Phillips threw his things into his bag, got into his car and headed for South Bend. He had 85 miles to go, just 85 miles. Somehow he felt that, as the end of his life's journey neared, it should be more than that.

He drove in darkness. No music, no talking to himself, no thinking. It was nearly midnight when he drove up the driveway at his mom and dad's house. A single light illuminated the living room behind the curtain. Phillips walked slowly to the door and opened it quietly.

His mother was asleep in the easy chair, a book open in front of her, the TV casting a bluish light on the room. He went up to her, whispered "Mom," then led her to her bed after a hug of greeting. Phillips went up to the bedroom and fell quickly asleep.

Hours later, he stirred. A ray of sunshine squeaked through the crack in the curtains, making a leafy pattern on the side of the dresser. Phillips lay there, watching it. From downstairs he smelled bacon and was sure that along with it would be three eggs over-easy, three slices of toast, maybe even some hash browns and pork and beans on the side. Funny how moms never forget.

"Tommy, come down for some breakfast," his mother called from the foot of the stairs, her voice a soft melody. "I made your favorite." For a brief moment, Phillips wondered to himself how he could even conceive of doing what he planned to in the house of this good woman, of these good people who had given him life, had nurtured him, had loved him without asking anything in return. He had no reply.

"Hi, Mom," Phillips said cheerfully as he walked into the kitchen, rubbing the sleep from his eyes. It looked to him like his mother had been up for hours yet was still as fresh as always. Maybe mothers never have to sleep?

"Tommy," she replied, rushed over and hugged him. "It's so wonderful to have you home again."

The kitchen, his mom, the breakfast were the same as always, wonderfully steadfast in a world that bragged of Internet time and hadn't the slightest notion or appreciation of timelessness.

"Your father is eager to see you, Tommy. Why not drive over after breakfast? I have lots to do today anyway and will keep plenty busy."

"Will do, Mom," Phillips answered as he savored the last bites of the eggs.

Phillips arrived at the nursing home a bit after 11. Visiting hours had just started, though whenever Phillips was in town the staff looked the other way regardless of when he showed up since they knew how much his dad loved the visits. He knocked lightly on his dad's door.

Joe looked up from the morning paper. "Tom. Nice to see you, Son."

Phillips walked over, bent to his dad in the wheelchair and they embraced. "Good trip?"

"Real good, Dad. I stopped off to see an old baseball buddy, Natalie, Kate and Uncle Matt and Aunt Millie."

"Did you now? That must have been wonderful seeing all of them within, what, a week?"

"Just about, Dad. Say, you look great."

"Thanks, Tom. You do too."

The two men, father and son, talked baseball, football, family, weather, children, this and that for 30 minutes more. Finally Joe fell silent and looked out the window. "Tom?"

"Yes, Dad, what's up?"

"Your mother came in here yesterday very worried and upset about you."

"She did?" Phillips was taken aback. "What did she say?"

"She said she has a feeling something is wrong." Joe turned to look directly at Phillips. "Is there?"

Phillips sat there silent.

"Well?"

"No, Dad, everything is fine."

Joe thought a moment, then sipped from a cup of coffee on the stand at the foot of his bed. "Son, I'm not going to get into a conversation of whether something is wrong or isn't. You're a grown man, and only you can be honest with yourself about your own life. But there are some things I want to say to you, have wanted to say and probably should have said by now."

Phillips listened.

"Tom, have you ever really looked around at the people in here? All of them, me, my roommate, the man across the hallway, down the hallway, around the corner, were once your age. Look in the mirror, Son. You see yourself, you see me.

"It goes quickly, Tom, believe me. It goes very quickly.

"Don't dwell on the bad in life, look for the good. You mean so much to your mother and me. You are a gift and a blessing, and our lives have been enriched immeasurably by your being. Son, there is such a fine line between happy and sad, blessed and desolate. I am happy at this moment, but if your mother died now, my life would fall apart.

"Find happiness yourself. You're not too old. Find the joy of being happily married to a woman, of having a family. Put down roots, whether in Indiana, Washington or wherever your heart leads you. You yourself wrote a book about unlikely happiness. For God's sake, why don't you listen to your own words?"

"You know about my book, Dad?"

"Tom, really. Do you honestly think your mother and I wouldn't find out about it? You were in every page of that book. And you know what?"

"What?"

"We're very proud of you."

Phillips smiled. Tears welled in his eyes. "Dad, thank you. I am happy you liked the book."

"And what about the rest?" Joe said.

"The rest of what?"

"Of what I said to you just now."

"I'll think on those things, Dad. Really I will."

"That's all I ask. That's all your mother and I can possibly ask. Just do the right thing."

Phillips got up, kissed his father goodbye and walked into the afternoon.

A note was on the kitchen table when he got back to his parents' house:

Tommy, I went to the grocery. Back in a little while, Mom.

He went outside and walked through the back yard. He playfully pushed the swing as he walked past. In the garden were Roma tomatoes, just like when he was growing up and Kate had in her own backyard now. The old birdhouse was still there, atop a pole and waiting for a new little family. He walked to a spot along the far reaches of the fence. In the shade were five graves. There were the first family dogs Mutt and Jeff, brother and sister cocker spaniels. Who would have thought that Jeff was the female? He chuckled at the thought and smiled at the boyhood memory of playing with the two of them as a tug of melancholy pulled at his heart with the everlasting sadness of their passing. Next to them was Maggie the

German shepherd, his mother's favorite, and the latecomer, Melanie the beloved chow, undoubtedly even now keeping watching over the house from her place in heaven. Nestled among them was the little cross Kate had made to mark the grave of Peepers, her one and only rooster. The cross was still implanted in the ground, its color now faded, its hardness now weakened, but its duty as a marker of one who had once been loved still in place.

Phillips sat on the grass amid the cherished memories. He warmed his face in the sun. Tomorrow would be his day of reckoning.

Chapter 20

Sandman

Phillips woke up on his own, no need or desire for an alarm clock on this, his last, day. The realization that he would be alive only another few hours felt strange to him because he didn't feel any differently than he had the day before or the week before. Shouldn't the prospect of death do weird things to the mind or make you reflective or sad or at least something? Who knew the answer to such a question? Phillips certainly didn't, nor did he intend to search for one.

One thing Phillips did know was that he had no wish to face his mother again or see Kate or anyone who might arrive at the house early. He took care of that by telling Mom he wanted to sleep in and skip breakfast and not come down until everyone was there. In his room, the one where he had spent his boyhood years dreaming of places yet to be and the person he wanted to become, Phillips would spend his final hours alone. Isn't that the way he had always liked it, independent, reliant on no one, he and his "it doesn't matters"? Phillips found these thoughts troubling now. They invaded his sense of order and sense of purpose and sense of righteousness about today. Could he be wrong? He tried not to entertain doubts, but he failed.

He took out a notebook to write a farewell letter but the words wouldn't come. How do you say goodbye to those you love when they would never be able to understand why you left when it was not your time, or left because you didn't want to ask for help when they would have been happy to do all they could for you?

A train sounded its whistle in the distance. Phillips walked over to the window and looked outside, hoping to catch another of its sounds, but the train was gone. Finally he took out his diary and began to write.

Saturday, July 15

I am here in my childhood bedroom, writing one last time. Funny I should even be doing this since I'll not be around to read it again years from now in a ripe old age. And I can't imagine those I love finding any solace in it, or meaning in it either. So I suppose I am doing it just because it might make me feel better about this. God, how I hate what I am about to do, but I see no other way. I'm sick and can't find a way out. The resolution I felt those many miles ago when I left Washington has now given way to a sense of resignation, making this more of an imperative than a choice. I spent time with friends and family, some with their own private hells. I don't hear about them planning to blow their brains out, so why I should be doing this? Then again, would they tell me if they were? Wouldn't it be just priceless if all of us ended up shooting ourselves at the same time, a sort of gang bang into eternity? God, I am a frivolous bastard. I can't even take my own death seriously. Actually, I think I am weak and full of crap and don't have the balls to take what life has to give, whether it be good or bad. I could have married Helena, but backed away. I suppose I could try and see if Maria and I got along, but I won't give that a chance either. I could have so much yet I try so little.

Dad and Father Luke, how they tried to talk sense into me and I won't listen. All I can say is that I walked toward the meadow but couldn't reach it. I looked for the sign but couldn't see it.

Phillips put down his pen. He had had enough of himself, and if he had the time or inclination, he figured he could always return to the diary later. Phillips took out the gun, unwrapped the towel from around it and loaded the chamber. Six bullets waiting. Which one would it be?

He spun the chamber, then put the barrel into his mouth. It tasted bitter, cold and final. Too messy this way, he thought to himself, and tried it instead pressed to his right temple. Ah, better. All he needed do now was wait for when the time was right.

Phillips heard guests arrive at the front door and move around the house. Helena. Bea, with the wedding rings in her purse. Phillips frowned. What in the world were they doing here? He heard Kate, Natalie, some long-time neighbors from up the street. Then Father Luke. His strong voice filled the living room from the front door and made its way to Phillips.

"Hello, Mrs. Phillips? I am Father Jonathan Luke, from Washington, D.C. Your son, Thomas, had invited me here today. I hope I am not making myself an imposition."

"An imposition? By all means no, Father," Peggy said. "Please come and join us. Tom told us you would be coming. My husband, Joe, will be over soon. A van is bringing him here from his nursing home."

"Mrs. Phillips, thank you for your kindness and your hospitality."

"Not at all, Father. I am delighted you could be here for our Tom's birthday."

Father Luke stopped abruptly. "His birthday? Today is Thomas's birthday?"

"Yes. My heavens, didn't he tell you?"

"As a matter of fact, no. I thought this was just a family get-together."

"That Tom, he can be something."

So this is why he wanted me to be here, Father Luke realized. He tilted his head upward and thought of Phillips, trying to connect spiritually with this searching soul.

"Father?" Peggy was looking at him.

"Yes, Mrs. Phillips?"

"Is everything alright?"

"Yes, Mrs. Phillips, everything is fine. I am pleased to be here with all of you. Somehow I feel Thomas will find the Lord this day, and he will find himself."

Peggy took Father Luke's hand and introduced him to her family and friends.

Phillips stood in the doorway of the bedroom with a wry smile. *So the timing comes out now, doesn't it? See? It's a perfect plan after all.* He wrote those final sentences in his diary and put it on the bed. Phillips walked over to his duffel bag again, reached inside for an envelope, opened it and took out Helena's card and began to read.

My Dear Tom: I'm sorry I can't be there for your birthday. Happy day and many wonderful returns! You know I will always, in my own special way, cherish the memory of what we had. Find happiness, Tom. You deserve it. I will be there for you. And just remember that a spot in my heart will be yours and only yours forever and ever and always. Love, Helena

Phillips smiled at the card and note, then stopped. "Why did she say she couldn't be here for my birthday and then she is? And what is Bea doing here?" Suddenly he feared they both sensed what he was going to do. Better hurry with this and get it over with.

But he wasn't ready, not quite yet.

He stepped out on the porch, returned inside and looked around the room. He went through the chest of drawers holding his keepsakes from decades and a lifetime ago. Feeling the wave of anxiety and anger come over him, he sat down again on the bed and for the one last time replayed the scene from his life-changing, and now life-ending, visit to the doctor's office.

The morning had passed, and it was time. He had come full circle. Raised in this room, now he would die in it, not so much because he wanted to die but more because he had found no reason to live. Phillips put his diary and Helena's card into the duffel bag, where he spotted the note for Helena he had written in D.C. and intended to mail here. Phillips dismissed the oversight with a shrug. "Getting sloppy late in life, aren't you?" he told himself with a grim chuckle.

He picked up the gun. How to do this?

Phillips leaned back against the pillows. It was too uncomfortable, so he returned to the edge of the bed, got up briefly to straighten the bedspread, adjusted himself to a relaxed position and took a deep breath. He tried again with the barrel of the gun in his mouth, thought better of it and pointed it at his temple.

His mind wandered. "Should I? Shouldn't I? Where is my resolve and sense of purpose? Gone, along with the other illusions I once held dear. Is everything just an illusion? Instead of building, do we instead just stay one step ahead of disaster? Was Dad right? Father Luke?

"Am I right?"

Phillips' family and friends prepared the birthday celebration. Gifts were piled on a card table in the dining room. The food was cooking. Peggy unboxed the cake she had ordered and put it on a plate, an heirloom she had inherited from her mother. She thought of the day 48 years ago when she had given birth to this wonderful man who had been a wonderful son. She could remember that day like it was only yesterday. And like that day all those years ago, Peggy was happy. Today her sandman was home.

Phillips cocked the pistol and pressed the barrel tightly to his head. He began to count.

10…Our Father…

9…who art in heaven…

8…hallowed be thy name…Peggy began to hum…

7…thy kingdom come…She went to the foot of the stairs and called. "Please hurry, Tommy, all the guests are here" …

6…thy will be done…

5…on earth asitisinheaven… Peggy began to sing. Her voice came up the stairs, the lullaby she had sung those many years ago. "Mr. Sandman, you sent me a dream"…

4…giveusthisdayourdailybreadandforgiveusourtrespasses…Phillips' breathing labored, his spirit cried out… "Oh, God, help me"…

3…"he is the cutest boy I've ever seen"…

2…Phillips blinked. A single drop of perspiration ran down his forehead, onto the tip of his nose and then to the bedspread. His mother continued singing, putting her own words to the tune she had loved from the first time she heard it those many decades ago.

Phillips put down the pistol, hung his head and started to cry. He folded his hands as if in prayer and balanced his chin on them. "Why did I stop?" he asked himself. "Was it fear? The song? Do I not have the guts to do this?" All he knew was that for whatever reason, or for utterly no reason at all, he didn't want to, couldn't go through with this.

Phillips uncocked the pistol, took out the bullets, wrapped the gun in the towel again and put it at the bottom of his duffel bag. He walked outside onto the porch.

The world was around him, and he looked and listened. A bird landed on the railing, turned its head to look at him, then took off. Dogs barked, children played. The apple tree he had loved as a boy grew there still, its branches reaching to the sky yet so close he could reach out and touch the leaves. In the living room and kitchen, his family and friends talked and waited. In other cities, with other people who were or were still to be in Phillips' path, life went on.

Taking in a deep breath, Phillips felt warmed by the summer afternoon. A light breeze tousled his hair and embraced him as he stood on the porch. If he could, he would have been content to stay there, savoring this day, enjoying the sunlight, wondering if he had seen the sign and where, rejoicing he had not pulled the trigger. But there would be time to think on those things. For now, he knew he had to go, first downstairs and later to whatever journey awaited him.

Phillips looked up into the sky and closed his eyes. Then, as he turned to go back inside, he spotted it. A beautifully formed ripening apple on a branch about two feet beyond the porch. "Can it be?" he said and knew it to be true. The sign had found him after all. And with that, Phillips smiled and looked around. He stepped near the railing, opened his zipper, took himself out, aimed and let loose with the stream.

Bull's-eye.